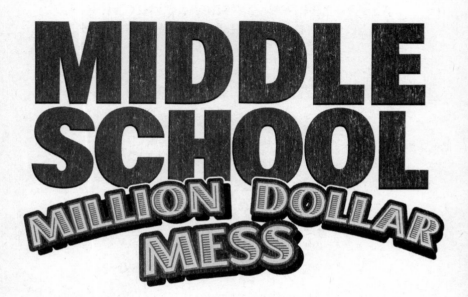

MIDDLE SCHOOL
MILLION DOLLAR MESS

JAMES PATTERSON

AND MARTIN CHATTERTON
ILLUSTRATED BY JOMIKE TEJIDO

JIMMY Patterson Books
LITTLE, BROWN AND COMPANY
NEW YORK • BOSTON

TO ALL THE MESSY FREAKS OUT THERE, AND ALSO TO THE ROAD WARRIOR, MRS. C —MC

Copyright © 2024 by James Patterson
Illustrations by Jomike Tejido

Cover art by Jomike Tejido.
Cover copyright © 2024 by Hachette Book Group, Inc.
Interior design by Michelle Gengaro-Kokmen.

JIMMY Patterson Books / Little, Brown and Company
Hachette Book Group
1290 Avenue of the Americas, New York, NY 10104
JamesPatterson.com

First Edition: January 2024

JIMMY Patterson Books is an imprint of Little, Brown and Company, a division of Hachette Book Group, Inc. The Little, Brown name and logo are trademarks of Hachette Book Group, Inc. The JIMMY Patterson Books® name and logo are trademarks of JBP Business, LLC.

The publisher is not responsible for websites (or their content) that are not owned by the publisher.

Little, Brown and Company books may be purchased in bulk for business, educational, or promotional use. For information, please contact your local bookseller or the Hachette Book Group Special Markets Department at special.markets@hbgusa.com.

Library of Congress Cataloging-in-Publication Data
Names: Patterson, James, 1947– author. | Chatterton, Martin, author. | Tejido, Jomike, illustrator.
Title: Million dollar mess / James Patterson and Martin Chatterton ; illustrated by Jomike Tejido.
Description: First edition. | New York : Little, Brown and Company, 2024. | Series: Middle school ; 16 | "JIMMY Patterson Books." | Summary: The Khatchadorian family discovers they have inherited a million dollars, but to get it, they must stay in a ramshackle house in Beverly Hills and Rafe has to attend a snooty new middle school.
Identifiers: LCCN 2023028514 | ISBN 9780316410625 (hardcover) | ISBN 9780316410724 (ebook)
Subjects: CYAC: Inheritance and succession—Fiction. | Wealth—Fiction. | Middle schools—Fiction. | Schools—Fiction. | Family life—Fiction. | Beverly Hills (Calif.)—Fiction.
Classification: LCC PZ7.P27653 Mil 2024 | DDC [Fic]—dc23
LC record available at https://lccn.loc.gov/2023028514

ISBNs: 978-0-316-41062-5 (hardcover), 978-0-316-41072-4 (ebook)

Printed in the United States of America

LSC-C

Printing 1, 2023

PROLOGUE

My name is Rafe Khatchadorian and I have something to confess. For almost two months straight this year, I got up in the morning and went out in public dressed like *this*.

Stuffy blazer

Sweater vest

Scratchy gray shorts

Regulation book bag

Starched socks

Shiny shoes

Take a good long look.

Go on. Have a laugh. Let it rip. I know you want to. *I* would, if I were you. *This* fancy costume is what I had to wear every day for two whole months.

Just take a second to think about that.

LOOK AT THAT VEST! *JUST LOOK AT IT!*

And, by the way, if this is what *you* have to wear for school in your universe, then I feel for you. I really, really do.

I'm not that old, but I've had some truly embarrassing moments in my life so far. There was the time I lost my swimsuit in the surf and washed up nude on a crowded beach.

That was pretty bad.

Then there was the time I was working at a fancy resort and drove this rich guy's boat and car right into the lake.

But this school uniform thing is—no contest— the single most embarrassing thing that's ever happened to me. Also, this has to stay between us, okay?

I'm trusting you not to show it to, say, Miller the Killer (my very own school bully), or Penelope

Deerwin (the girl I sort of, maybe, have a crush on), or, you know, ANY OTHER HUMAN BEING.

Of course, this uniform wasn't at *my* school. Imagine trying to get Miller the Killer to dress like that! No, I was wearing this uniform because—Wait! Hold on a minute, I'm getting ahead of myself. Let's start this particular Rafe Khatchadorian adventure back at the point where it *really* began, which was on one rainy Tuesday afternoon...

CHAPTER 1

RAIN, RAIN, GO AWAY

Okay. We can all agree there is *nothing* in the world as boring as a rainy day stuck at home. It's more boring than watching a sloth climb a fifty-foot tree. Or a ten-foot tree. Who am I kidding—even a shrub. More boring than pretending to listen to Principal Stricker lecture me on school rules and regulations.

I was so bored that even Wormhole wasn't doing it for me.

Usually, Grandma Dotty is around to make sure Georgia doesn't completely trash the house while Mom's at work, but today, she'd gone out with her friends and left me in control. Me!

I mean, that's just plain irresponsible. Didn't

she know my history of turning completely simple situations into full-blown war zones?

Q: How selfish can one grandma be?

A: Very selfish.

So there I was, minding my own business, watching TV, when...

Bzzt!

"The weather today is rainy and cold, with an eighty percent chance of more rain—"

Bzzt!

"The sloth lazes about, with no friends and nothing to do—"

I opened my eyes from my nap to see my incredibly annoying little sister, Georgia, doing what she does best: *being incredibly annoying*.

Without even asking me, she was channel-surfing the TV with about a zillion of her annoying little friends.

"Hey!" I yelled. "I was watching that movie!"

"You were asleep," Georgia replied without turning around. "And anyway, *we* don't like the Avengers. Do we, girls?"

"Yeah? Well, I do. Turn it back on."

Georgia's friends all hissed at me. At once. It was terrifying. I don't mind admitting that I immediately abandoned all hope of seeing the rest of the movie.

As Georgia and her crew began screeching along with YouTube singing sensation Devlin Beaver, I rolled off the couch, moved to the window, and wiped some fog off the glass.

It was raining hard outside. Hills Village

never looks its best in the rain, and today was no exception.

Usually, if I'm bored—like NOW—I start drawing or doing something artistic. But for some completely unknown reason, I'd lost my mojo.

It was gone. Vanished. It was no more. I was mojo-less.

Every time I picked up a pencil or a paintbrush I ended up staring at the blank piece of paper for hours. This was a big problem. All artists need their mojo, and I didn't know if mine would ever come back.

I was so bored, I wished anything would happen. It didn't need to be a good anything, just as long as there was a *something*.

A flaming meteorite landing on Hills Village. Space aliens.

A zombie invasion.

ANYTHING!

But let's face it, nothing was going to happen.

Life doesn't work like that. It would just keep raining, and raining, and raining, until—

KNOCK! KNOCK! KNOCK!

CHAPTER 2

SHARK, LEECH, ATO & GOUGE

It tells you how bad things had gotten when I reacted to a knock at the door like this:

Woo-hoo!

In the 0.2 seconds it took for me to wrench open the door, a few possibilities flashed through my mind.

A. We had won the lottery. This was extremely unlikely, mainly because Mom never entered the lottery.
B. The government was in trouble and needed a new superspy. This was also extremely unlikely.
C. Penelope had come to beg me to go to the movies with her. Off-the-charts unlikely, seeing as she was currently in Timbuktu with her mom, a veterinarian who traveled all over the world.
D. None of the above.

When I opened the door, all I found was a red-haired man in a gray suit.

"Rafe Khatchadorian?" the man said.

"Who wants to know?" I said.

I didn't say that. If I were in a movie, I might have said that. But I wasn't, so I didn't.

"Uh, yeah," I said. "I'm he—him. I mean, that's I.

Rafe, me, he. I'm he. Rafe is me. Yeah. Totally."

It had been a long day. You ever get that when faced with conversations with grown-ups? They say something that isn't a question and you say something majorly dumb right back without thinking about what you're saying? As if your mouth starts talking before your brain tells it what to say.

No? Just me? Where were we?

"Okay," the man in gray said slowly. He handed me a business card. "My name is Thomas Ato."

No way.

"Tom Ato?" I said, glancing at his hair and trying not to smile. "Hey, maybe we should *ketchup* sometime?"

"Yes, very amusing. I don't think I've ever heard anyone make *that* joke before. I am a lawyer, Mr. Khatchadorian, representing the firm of Shark, Leech, Ato, and Gouge. We have been trying to get in touch with you for some weeks, but our letters have gone unanswered. Is your mother in?"

"No," I said. "She won't be back until six."

"Well, when she does get home, please ask her to call my office for a face-to-face meeting so we can discuss the matter further." He sniffed and turned to leave.

"Wait, that's it?" I said. "You're going to leave me hanging?"

Tom Ato hesitated. "I'm afraid the parameters of my profession and the legislation thereof legally prevent any officer of the court from divulging anything *vis-à-vis* the matter at hand at this juncture."

I just blinked at him.

"I've got some good news and I've got some bad news," he said. "That's all I can say."

He walked down the pathway, got into his car (no prizes for guessing the color), and drove away, leaving me doing an impression of a puzzled guppy (see illustration for details).

CHAPTER 3

ASSAULT WITH A DEADLY EGGPLANT

The rest of that day passed even more slowly than it had before Tom Ato had dropped his bombshell. I waited until Mom got home and started to make dinner before I mentioned Mr. Ato.

"Thomas Ato? Tom Ato?" Mom cocked her head to one side. "You're kidding."

"He's not an actual tomato. He's a lawyer."

"A lawyer?"

"Yeah. People who deal with the law? You must have heard of them," I said. "They're always on TV."

Mom gave a short laugh and threw a piece of eggplant at me. It bounced off my head and fell to the floor, where Junior snatched it up.

"Hey! I'm pretty sure that's against the law," I said. "Eggplant assault."

"You can check with your new fruit-and-vegetable expert tomorrow," Mom said. She continued chopping. "I wonder what he wants?"

"Maybe he found out Georgia was adopted," I said. "And we aren't actually related."

"And what's the bad news?" Georgia said triumphantly.

She and Mom high-fived each other right in front of me, which I thought was pretty rude. Still, I had to admit, it was a zinger.

Nothing else happened, so I'll stop this chapter right here.

CHAPTER 4

DEATH BY WHALE?

Only Mom and I went to see Mr. Ato. Mom said Grandma Dotty had to stay to make sure Georgia didn't have a party or something. I wasn't complaining. In fact, I was dying to know exactly what the good news was. I kinda pushed the bad news way down in a corner and didn't think about what it might be.

How bad could it be?

"The bad news," Mr. Ato said, when we were seated in front of his desk in his office, "is that one of your relatives has passed away."

Okay, that's pretty bad.

Mom frowned. "But I don't have all that many relatives. I'm sure I'd know if I were missing one…"

Mr. Ato pulled a sheet of paper toward him and

peered down at it. "Well, it seems your husband's father's half brother, Grey Aloysius Vernon Khatchadorian, has departed."

My head was starting to hurt. Mom's husband's father's half brother?

"I never knew Grandpa Khatchadorian had a brother!" Mom said.

"It seems so," Mr. Ato replied solemnly. "Families are very complicated these days."

"Amen," I said, thinking about my own dad. I'm too lazy to explain now—especially if I start adding in husbands' fathers' half brothers—but full details are available in *Middle School: Get Me Out of Here!*

"Why don't we just call him Uncle Grey to make things easier?" Mr. Ato said. "I mean, it's not strictly accurate, but at this point it doesn't really matter."

Mom and I both nodded.

"Your uncle died several months ago, but it has taken this long to find out where you lived. He died in California and had no other relatives. Rafe is his only blood relative remaining."

I blinked. I wasn't too sure about that

"remaining" part. It made me sound like my days were numbered.

"California?" Mom said.

Mr. Ato nodded. "Beverly Hills, California."

"How did he die?" Mom asked. "Old age?"

"Ah, no, unfortunately not, Mrs. Khatchadorian. Your uncle was eaten by a whale during a surfing lesson."

All three of us fell silent as we contemplated Uncle Grey's gory and surprising end.

Given how close I'd come to being whale chum just a couple of months ago while in Alaska with Penelope and Dr. Deerwin, I definitely felt for him.

What can I say? I've got a taste for Khatchadorians.

Burp!

"Hey," I said, recovering quickly—don't judge me; I never knew I even *had* a sort-of uncle until two minutes ago—"what's the good news?"

"Oh yes, I almost forgot." Mr. Ato lifted a file from his tray. "Rafe has inherited a house. Mr. Khatchadorian left him everything. Of course, as Rafe is a minor, you'll have to look after the legal side of things, Mrs. Khatchadorian."

"A *house?*" I repeated. "Whoa! How much is it worth?"

"Rafe! Don't be so rude!" Mom said. "Think about poor old Uncle Grey!" She leaned forward and looked at the lawyer. "How much *is* it worth, though?"

Mr. Ato handed Mom a sheet of paper. "It's difficult to say, Mrs. Khatchadorian, but from what I can see, it won't be much less than a million dollars."

A MILLION BUCKS!

CHAPTER 5

THERE IS ONE CONDITION

A million bucks! A *million*!

I'd seen ten thousand dollars before when I got a reward for catching a wanted poacher in Alaska (which you can read all about in *Middle School: Winter Blunderland*)—but I couldn't even *picture* a million!

It was all I could do to stop myself from kissing Mr. Ato.

Mom didn't—stop herself, I mean. She leaped right across the desk and planted a big wet smacker on the lawyer's shiny forehead. Mr. Ato turned the color of, well, a tomato.

"This isn't a joke, right?" Mom said, still holding Mr. Ato's head. "Because that wouldn't be very funny."

Mr. Ato wriggled out of Mom's clutches and straightened his tie. "I am not in the habit of joking about matters like this, Mrs. Khatchadorian. The house is number 322 Chestnut Drive, Beverly Hills, California."

I'd been to California before, but that trip had been way different than I'd hoped it would be. Instead of seeing Hollywood, we'd gone camping in the middle of nowhere. It seemed that this time, I was finally going to get the trip I'd been dreaming about!

Plus, in my head I was thinking about all the things we could do with a million dollars. Big red sports car, check. Guitar-shaped swimming pool, check.

Summer vacation in, oh, let's say Barbados…

I could see myself in a hammock hitched between two gently swaying palm trees while—

Mr. Ato coughed. "There is one condition."

Sports car, pool, and Barbados vanished. Ditto with the palm trees.

"Condition?" Mom said.

I sensed that what he was about to say would involve trouble for someone—most likely me.

I wasn't wrong.

"Your uncle insisted that, to inherit 322 Chestnut Drive, you and your family must live there for a minimum of two months and that both you and your sister must attend *his* old school for a semester—Beverly Hills Preparatory School in Beverly Hills, where he was class president. The estate will pay for your airfares and the school fees. BHP is a very exclusive school."

"That's it?" I asked. "All we have to do is go to California and stay there for two months, while I go to a fancy-schmancy school, and we get the house?"

Mr. Ato nodded. Mom looked happy.

"Easy," I said, smiling like an idiot.

This was before I found out about the uniform.

CHAPTER 6

OFFENDERS WILL BE FED
TO THE SCHOOL TIGER

N o. No way. Not a chance. Forget it. Not gonna happen. Nuh-uh." I shook my head firmly. This was nonnegotiable. Rafe Khatchadorian was not a man to be messed with. There was no way I was agreeing to *this*. California was off the table.

"*I hate you!*" Georgia wailed. "I wanna go to Beverly Hills!"

"But it's a *million dollars*," Mom said. "And it's just a uniform."

"Yeah!" Georgia shouted. "It's just a *uniform*, Mr. Selfish!"

I looked at them both coolly and raised an eyebrow (it's hard to do, by the way—raise one eyebrow, I mean—I'd practiced for months to get it right just for moments like these) and pointed a quivering finger at the computer screen, where the Beverly Hills Prep's school uniform was displayed in all its horrific glory: the sweater vest, the starched socks, the jacket, the *necktie*.

"Does that look like 'just a uniform'?" I said. "I don't think so."

"I still hate you!" Georgia yelled.

"I'm sure you don't have to wear all of the uniform," Mom said.

"'Beverly Hills Preparatory School operates a very strict uniform code,'" I read aloud. "'No exceptions. Offenders will be fed to the school tiger.'"

Mom's eyes almost popped out of their sockets. "What?!"

"Okay, I made up that last bit," I said. "But I'm still absolutely, definitely, totally, one hundred and ten percent NOT doing it."

CHAPTER 7

THE HOUSE ON CHESTNUT DRIVE

Back in Hills Village, when Mr. Ato had told us we'd inherited a house in Beverly Hills, I'd gone online and found that the neighborhood looked pretty ritzy.

If you're wondering what changed my mind about going to California and wearing that horrifying uniform, the answer is simple. Mom just *told* me I was going, and deep down I didn't blame her one little bit. A million bucks is a million bucks. That's a whole bunch of shifts at Swifty's Diner for Mom. My dignity didn't stand a chance against that.

But one flight to California later, when we pulled up outside something that could have come straight out of a horror movie, I asked the taxi driver to double-check the address. I'd looked on Google before we left, but the place had been hidden by a big truck.

"This is it, no mistake—322 Chestnut Drive." The taxi driver glanced nervously at the house and shuddered. "Good luck."

There were only the three of us: me, Mom, and Georgia. Grandma Dotty had offered to stay behind to look after the house, and besides, someone had to dog-sit Junior.

Within three seconds, the taxi driver had dumped our bags on the sidewalk and zipped off in a cloud of exhaust. I stared at the rusty iron gate. It had the letters G. K. spelled out in wrought iron, and my heart sank. The taxi driver was right. This was Uncle Grey's place. A screeching bird on top of the gate peered at us like we were breakfast. It screeched once and then flapped off to settle on the roof of our new house.

"There's got to be some mistake," Mom said.

Georgia burst into tears. I was grateful she'd done that because it stopped me from doing the exact same thing.

The garden looked like the weeds had a meeting one day and decided to strangle the house. If I said it was a jungle, that wouldn't be fair to regular, tidy jungles like the Amazon and, er, other famous jungles. Scattered in the twisting, wriggling weeds was an impressive collection of total junk.

I figured there were probably a couple of dead bodies and some radioactive nuclear waste hidden somewhere in there, too, but I wasn't in any hurry to look closer without a hazmat suit and gas mask.

The windows that weren't smashed were covered in a thick layer of dust. The roof sagged in more places than it didn't. Rooms seemed to have been added by a do-it-yourself enthusiast with a thing for Count Dracula. To top it all off, the house was rammed right underneath a HUGE freeway halfway through construction. A thick cloud of concrete dust drifted down from a jackhammer clattering away about three inches from Uncle Grey's chimney.

"It might be better inside!" Mom shouted. I gave her the famous Rafe Khatchadorian Eyebrow Raise.

"Oh, right!" I shouted back. "Because I really like the outside!"

I was being sarcastic.

In case you hadn't guessed.

CHAPTER 8

WEREWOLVES OF BEVERLY HILLS

Mom gave me the key and pointed at the front door.

"Me?" I squeaked, trying and failing to keep the tremor of TOTAL FEAR out of my voice. "You want me to go in first?"

Mom nodded. "Uh-huh."

I gulped and tried to think of a way I could avoid opening the door without looking like a complete scaredy-cat. Hadn't Mom seen *any* scary movies?

Whoever goes into a spooky house first *always* gets nabbed. A rookie error. There was no *way*—No, wait.

I'd gotten that wrong. It's always the kid at the *back* who's the first to go.

I looked around to check that Georgia was last in line. Good. If the house was full of zombies or vampires or guys wearing hockey masks, it'd be Georgia they'd go for. Call me heartless, but hey, better her than me, right?

I turned the key and pushed the door, which creaked inward slowly on rusty hinges. I couldn't see a thing inside the house. I stepped through the doorway...and walked straight into a thick blanket of cobwebs.

Have you ever seen anyone do that? Walk into a spiderweb, I mean? Hilarious, isn't it?

Unless it happens to you.

I screamed so loud I drowned out the jackhammers, whirling around and around, scrabbling at my face like a wild man before the *GIANT MUTANT SPIDER* sank its giant mutant fangs into my neck.

Okay, here's the thing. After having a giant mutant spider land on your neck, you'd have been kinda safe to assume *that* was probably going to be the worst thing that happened to you on that particular day, wouldn't you? Which just goes to show how wrong you can be because, as I streaked blindly across the room, I slammed straight into a werewolf.

Yep, you heard me: a werewolf.

Big, hairy beast with massive sharp claws and a mouth full of razor-sharp teeth? You know what I mean. A WEREWOLF.

Now, I'm not looking for sympathy here—okay, I am—but what would *you* do if, one after the other, you:

1. had gotten a face full of sticky-icky cobwebs;
2. were about to have a giant mutant spider inject you with venom; and
3. had just run into a werewolf in a haunted house?

Exactly. I fainted.

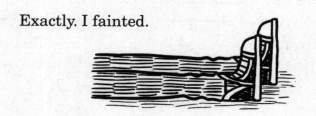

CHAPTER 9

TALKING COCKROACHES

When the mists cleared, a giant moon was looking at me.

"Rafe woke up, Mom!" yelled the moon, which, for some weird reason, had the exact same voice as Georgia.

The moon face disappeared and my eyes focused.

I lifted my head to find I was lying on a huge moldy couch in what must have been Uncle Grey's house...only, now it had the lights on. Mom was moving around the room, lifting dust sheets off things and turning on lamps. Personally, I was a little annoyed that she wasn't, y'know, mopping my brow with a cold towel and looking all sympathetic and motherly.

"Where is it?" I whispered.

Mom stopped in her tracks. "Where's what, honey?"

"The werewolf!"

"Oh." Mom pointed behind me. "There."

Georgia says I jumped about forty-six feet in the air, but I know she's exaggerating because the ceiling was only nine feet high and I hit that.

There, behind the couch, was the werewolf.

Except it wasn't. It was a stuffed bear. A kind of

mangy, moth-eaten stuffed bear with one eye and some of its stuffing leaking out of one leg.

"How are you feeling?" Mom asked.

I dropped back down to the couch, using my special ninja skills. "Take a wild guess."

As most of you know, I don't have any special ninja skills, so I bounced off the couch and landed safely on the floor, cleverly using my face to cushion my fall. As Georgia and Mom laughed like it was the funniest thing they'd ever seen, I just lay on the shag carpet and watched a giant cockroach walk slowly across my nose.

From where I was lying, that "good news" part of the deal Mr. Ato had mentioned wasn't looking so good.

CHAPTER 10

WARNING!
ART TALK AHEAD!

Okay, I admit it, the cockroach didn't say anything.

And if I'm being totally honest? There wasn't even a cockroach.

But there *should* have been, because the inside of Uncle Grey's house—*our* house now, I guess— was even more trashed than the outside. If there'd been a *swarm* of cockroaches, it wouldn't have surprised me. There was stuff everywhere.

Boxes of smelly books and papers were piled high in teetering stacks around the living room like a mountain range. There seemed to be about twice as much furniture as anyone would ever need and almost all of it was broken in some way:

the padding leaking out of a split seam here, a quivering spring waiting for some unsuspecting butt there. Behind the couch was the giant stuffed bear, but you already know about that. There were a few more stuffed animals dotted around, too—a moldy old crow, a creepy-looking bat, a giant moose head with its antlers painted bright green. I'm guessing Uncle Grey wasn't exactly what you'd call an animal lover. And after working with animals with Penelope and Dr. Deerwin for so long, I kind of felt bad for the moose head.

And then there were the paintings—hundreds of them—big ones, small ones, square ones, and tall ones.

They were stacked and racked against the walls and furniture in rows six deep. Every inch of wall space was covered, and it was clear that they were pretty much all painted by the same person.

"Ewww," Georgia said, peering at one of the biggest, which hung at an angle above the dusty mantelpiece. "What is *that* supposed to be?"

"It's not supposed to be anything," I said. "It's an abstract, just like Mom's paintings."

"It stinks," Georgia said, before losing interest and wandering off toward what looked like the kitchen.

I stared at the painting and suddenly forgot all about werewolves and broken furniture.

The drumming of jackhammers from the freeway overhead faded away.

Looking at the painting was like staring into deep space. A thick swirl of blue paint on a darker blue background was crisscrossed and dotted all over with splashes and marks of yellow and green and lilac. Thin trickles of paint danced crazily across the canvas, as though a drunk mouse had fallen into a can of paint and then set off home, dragging its tail behind it. For all I knew, that was exactly what had happened. This thing was a complete and total mess, an explosion in a paint factory, a peek inside a fantastically mixed-up mind. I loved it. Whoever had painted this was a genius. Georgia didn't know her Picasso from her El Greco.

I dragged a footstool over and stood on it to straighten the painting. As I did, I noticed a signature scrawled in a corner: *G. Khatchadorian, 10.11.1987.*

Uncle Grey was the genius!

CHAPTER 11

THE WORST DAY OF MY LIFE

I'll come back to the painting stuff later (believe me, there's plenty more to tell) and I'll also give you more info on 322 Chestnut Drive (plenty more there, too).

But right now let's deal with Beverly Hills Prep.

Remember how I showed you that lousy school uniform at the start of this story? And how Mr. Ato told us about 322 Chestnut Drive coming with a few conditions? Well, one of those conditions was that I had to attend Uncle Grey's old school, Beverly Hills Preparatory School, and that uniform is what I had to wear. No BHP = no 322 Chestnut Drive.

After almost strangling myself with the tie, I came downstairs. Georgia and Mom both looked at me and then at each other.

"Not. A. Word," I said, and held up a finger.

Mom gave Georgia one of those laser-death-ray stares and I knew she was doing a mind-meld on her NOT to laugh.

Georgia—whose girls' uniform was a TOTALLY NORMAL skirt and button-down polo—looked like her head was going to explode with the effort of keeping a straight face. "You look…nice," she said in a strangled voice.

I grabbed a piece of toast and slunk out. "Have a good day, Rafe," Mom called.

I closed the door of 322 Chestnut Drive behind me and, before I made it to the gate, I heard the muffled sound of hysterical laughter from inside the house.

CHAPTER 12

WELCOME TO
BEVERLY HILLS PREP!

Beverly Hills Prep was right around the corner from Uncle Grey's house, so I didn't have far to go.

That was the only good thing about it. That and the fact that no one I actually knew was around to see my shame.

Mom, Georgia, and I had gone online and checked out exactly where the school was the day before so we knew where we were going, except Georgia's classes were in the south wing of the school and mine were in the north. I saw about a trillion people on the way, but none of them gave me a second glance. As I approached the school, I began to see other kids dressed the same as me.

Some shot me snotty looks, and I heard a few of them saying stuff about me. So far it was pretty much like Hills Village Middle School.

I rounded the corner and got my first look at BHP.

It was huge.

It was ritzy.

It was—

I didn't get to finish my thought because a kid stuck out a leg and I fell headfirst into an ornamental bush.

When I untangled myself, I looked up to see three kids laughing at me—not with me, in case you were wondering. Definitely *at* me. There's a difference.

"You need to watch where you're going, dork," said a tall kid with the cleanest hair I'd ever seen. I mean, this dude's hair could have been in a shampoo ad, it was so clean. In fact, now that I looked at him more closely, *everything* about him was kinda shiny: shiny clothes, shiny hair, shiny— well, you get the picture.

"Yeah," I said, hauling myself out of the bush and picking a leaf out of my ear.

It wasn't the *snappiest* comeback I'd ever come up with.

It wasn't really a comeback at all, if I'm being totally honest.

The three shiny BHP kids laughed. They had me pegged as a major BHP loser *and I hadn't even gotten through the school gate.* Even for Rafe Khatchadorian, this was a record.

"Is your tie *supposed* to be bunched up like that?" Captain Shiny Hair asked. The way he said it, it sounded like he already knew the answer, but I wasn't about to give him the satisfaction.

"Yeah," I replied. "Is your hair *supposed* to be so shiny?" Again, you'll notice, I didn't have much in the way of snappy comebacks.

"Why, yes, actually," Captain Shiny Hair said. He flipped his shiny hair.

His two little cronies smirked.

"And if you're thinking of actually attending BHP dressed like that," Captain Shiny Hair sneered, "you'll need to do something about your appearance. We have *standards* at this school, you know."

My appearance? What did he mean? I was dressed more properly than I'd ever been dressed in my life. Okay, I may have had half a bush sticking to my rear end and enough twigs in my hair to light a campfire, but still...

"Five uniform demerits!" a voice behind me shouted, and I jumped about nine feet in the air.

Captain Shiny Hair and his team moved toward the school, snickering. I turned to see a teacher looking at me like I was a particularly nasty pile of dog doo-doo.

"Report to the office immediately!" the teacher barked.

Grr!

I knew he was a teacher because:

1. he wore one of those jackets with leather patches on the elbows; and
2. he had a face that looked like a rat sucking a lemon.

"Name?" he barked.

"Rafe Khatchadorian?" I have no idea why I said it like I wasn't sure myself. Chalk it up to nerves. In my defense, I was wearing a sweater vest and necktie in public. My concentration levels were at just about the lowest they'd ever been.

The teacher had eyebrows so wild and bushy they reminded me of the garden at 322 Chestnut Drive. He had a mustache to match. I half expected to spot a rusting car buried in the hairy undergrowth on his top lip. "Ten language demerits!" he barked. "Failed to use 'sir' when addressing a teacher!"

Without another word, he turned and marched through the school gates, looking as though he wanted to invade a small country.

I sagged and let out a long sigh. It wasn't even school time and I already wanted to go home.

A big kid in a BHP uniform walked past.

He had a sad face and a shaggy head of bright red hair.

"See you met the Winners Club," he said. "And Mr. Fitzpatrick."

"What?" I said, brushing dirt off my bare knees. I shook my head. *The Winners Club?*

"You'll learn," the big kid said, and lumbered off as the bell sounded for the start of my first day at BHP.

CHAPTER 13

SAY ELEPHANT!
DON'T SAY ELEPHANT!

By lunchtime, I had been issued nineteen more demerits. The only teacher who hadn't given me one was the art teacher, Ms. Bennett, who seemed almost human. Exactly what she was doing at BHP I had no idea.

In the non–Ms. Bennett lessons, I collected nine uniform demerits.

I got five more language demerits (all for insufficient "sirring"), three

Wonky tie

Shirttail untucked

Muddy shorts

Leaf on butt

Socks too saggy

Dust on shoes

demerits for violations of something called "school spirit" (no, I had no clue, either), and a demerit from a passing velociraptor who I later discovered was Principal Winton, simply because he didn't like the expression on my face. Which was kind of ironic because I didn't like the expression on his face, either. I also got a demerit for not shouting "Elephant!"—I'll explain later.

The only good thing about all of this was that I had absolutely no idea what a lousy demerit was. It didn't *sound* good, but for now, there didn't seem to be any other consequences to my rule-breaking. I thought back to Hills Village Middle School and my campaign to break every rule in the schoolbook. If I tried *that* at BHP, I'd be at it until I was sixty-five. Alongside all the usual stuff about phones and gum and bullying, there were rules about which side of the hallway you could walk on, what color socks could be worn on the second Thursday in April, the correct way to eat soup, a ban on breathing through your mouth…you get the picture. There was even a weird one that involved yelling the word *elephant* if a teacher told the class to be quiet. I'm not kidding—the second period

I was in, there was a bit too much chatter going on and the teacher said, "Quiet!" Immediately, everyone stood up and yelled "Elephant!" Then they sat down.

I hadn't moved because I'd figured everyone had gone nuts and I was scoping out the nearest exit.

Which was why I got a demerit for not saying "elephant."

There was no way I was going to make it through the next two months.

CHAPTER 14

BIG DORK MOMENT COMING UP

I was exhausted. Beat. Done. Pooped.

Keeping hold of 322 Chestnut Drive depended on me staying put at BHP, and if this morning was anything to go by, I didn't know if I had it in me.

I trudged over to the cafeteria, which looked pretty much like the dining hall at Hogwarts. I had no appetite, but if I was going to make it through the first day I needed to keep up my strength.

I waited in line with my tray and took my lunch across to an empty seat in the middle of the enormous room. I noticed a few kids looking in my direction, but none of them seemed too friendly.

The empty seat I'd spotted was next to the big

redheaded kid with the sad face, who, so far, had been the only BHP student besides Captain Shiny Hair to speak to me all morning. He glanced up as I walked over to him.

"Okay if I sit here?" I asked.

The big kid looked like he'd just been told he had two days to live. "Uh, yeah," he said, after a pause. "I guess so."

14 years later...

I sat down miserably.

Was there a rule about where to position my fork and knife?

I looked at Big Red's place setting. He probably

had a name, but I was just going to call him Big Red from now on. He'd already picked up his fork and knife to eat; pinkie up, of course. I spotted the Velociraptor across the hall with Mr. Fitzpatrick, his mustache stalking the edges of the room, waiting to pounce on anyone who so much as breathed out of place.

"This place is *complicated*," I said to Big Red.

Big Red nodded slowly and chewed his food. He looked like an orangutan munching on bamboo, or whatever it is orangutans eat. He opened his mouth to say something and I waited for the words to come out.

"Yeah," he said, and took another chomp of his lunch.

It wasn't exactly sparkling conversation, but it was the only option I had. I noticed Captain Shiny Hair staring at me and I asked Big Red about him.

"Oh," Big Red said. "Him."

I waited patiently. I was getting used to Big Red's way of (not) speaking.

"Cory Tamworth-Blythe," Big Red said. He chewed for about a month before speaking again. "His dad's Henry Tamworth-Blythe. Rich. Gives

money. A lot. To the school. Also…" Big Red took
another bite. Chew. Wait. Chew. Wait. Chew. Wait.

Tumbleweed

"Also?" I said encouragingly, in case Big Red
took another bite and I lost the will to live.

"Also an idiot."

I was just about to say something else when I
heard the Velociraptor tell the room to be quiet.

Not wanting to get another demerit, I jumped
to my feet and yelled, "Elephant!"

I realized something was wrong right away.

I'm smart like that.

The entire dining room—a quick head count
told me there were about, oh, 182,624 kids in
total—stared at me, open-mouthed. Captain Shiny
Hair was looking like Christmas had come early
and I was his gift-wrapped present.

If my time at BHP had *any* chance of working out, I was pretty sure this little mistake had just squashed that completely. I wasn't just a weird new kid, I was the weird new kid who stood up and shouted "Elephant!"

Way worse.

Or better, depending on who you were.

I sat down and picked up my fork and knife.

"Two demerits!" the Velociraptor yelled. "Inappropriate shouting of 'elephant'!"

"Oh boy," Big Red muttered, and scooted away from me, as though my dorkiness might be contagious.

He was probably right.

CHAPTER 15

I AM AN OMELET

I'll skip the horror of the rest of day one.

The main thing you need to know is, by the time lunch was over, my nickname was Elephant Boy.

As soon as the bell sounded, I headed across the *gigantic* sports fields. I was making for the trees that bordered the running track. This, Big Red had told me, was the back way out of school.

The route took me past a small house with its own garden. I figured it belonged to the school caretaker—I'd seen a guy in green overalls driving around on a golf cart towing a trailer of gardening tools. He'd waved at me, so, by BHP standards, the caretaker was my best friend.

I rounded the corner and noticed a group of

kids throwing something at the back of the house.

It was Captain Shiny Hair, aka Cory Tamworth-Blythe, and his minions. The Winners Club (*gag*) had a carton of eggs and were throwing them at the windows of the caretaker's house.

"Hey!" I yelled, without thinking.

A little voice inside my head said, *What do you think you're doing? Hasn't today been bad enough without getting stomped on, too?*

The voice was right, but it was too late. I got ready to be stomped.

To my surprise, the Winners Club took one look at me and ran for the trees.

I blinked.

Maybe my massive haul of demerits had somehow catapulted me to instant "bad boy" status?

"Yeah!" I yelled (although not too loudly in case they turned around and came back to pummel me; I didn't have a plan for that). "You better run!"

I jogged over to the carton of eggs and shook my fist at their departing backs. I picked up the eggs and looked around for a garbage bin. The Khatchadorians may be many things, but we're no litterers.

"Hey!" a voice said. "You!"

I turned to see a girl about my age, wearing shorts and a T-shirt and the exact same expression as an MMA fighter about to enter the cage. She had come out of the caretaker's house and was heading my way fast.

I looked down at the egg carton and back at the house that was covered in eggs. The Winners Club had disappeared.

"Ah," I said, holding up a finger. "Okay, I see

what you're thinking, but there's an explanation
for all this. You see—"

That was as far as I got because the girl did two
things at what seemed to be super-ninja speed.

First, she grabbed an egg and cracked it over
my head. Then she kicked me in the shin.

"Ow! Hey!" I yelped, hopping on the spot and
trying to see through the film of egg white that
now covered my face.

The girl cracked another egg and kicked me in
the other shin.

"I didn't throw any—*Ow!*"

She repeated her egg-cracking, shin-kicking
routine. It was one she was clearly happy with
because she was sticking to it. Crack, kick, repeat.
Crack, kick, repeat.

I hopped away, still trying to explain that it wasn't me who'd been throwing the eggs while she just kept right on cracking and kicking, kicking and cracking. She was *good* at it, too. Accurate.

Accurate angle

Speed of foot

Eventually, just as I was running out of unbruised shin, I turned and sprinted for the trees. To my relief, she didn't keep up the chase.

With egg on my face—literally—and with my shins throbbing like a nuclear power plant, I limped painfully back home.

The jackhammers on the freeway were still

hard at work. It was warm out. The concrete dust drifted down onto the slowly cooking egg. By the time I reached the front door and staggered inside, I looked like a cement-coated omelet.

"How was your day at Bev—?" Mom put her hand to her mouth. I must have looked bad because even Georgia didn't say anything funny.

"Put it this way," I said, scooping a handful of cooked egg off my nose, "I've had it with elephants."

CHAPTER 16

THE SURVIVAL PLAN

It took all my powers of persuasion to stop Mom from IMMEDIATELY heading to BHP and getting the egg-cracking, shin-kicking girl arrested.

Don't get me wrong: I wasn't too happy about being turned into an omelet with bruised shins, but on top of being named Elephant Boy on my very first day, if I came in on day two with Mom in tow, my life at BHP would be over. And if that happened, we could kiss the million bucks good-bye.

"I'll be fine," I said to Mom. "Let me handle it."

I *sounded* confident. I *sounded* like I knew how to handle myself. The trouble was, I had literally NO IDEA how I was going to force myself back into BHP after everything that had happened.

Based on day one, Mr. Fitzpatrick was probably going to be waiting at the gates for me armed with nuclear weapons.

"Lyle bakes your face off right, old skinner," Mom said. "Murders and flies?"

"Huh?" I yelled over the sound of the jackhammers. Had I driven her over the edge?

"I *said*," Mom screeched, "I'll make your favorite for dinner! Burgers and fries?"

I nodded. "Anything except eggs," I said, and headed upstairs to de-omelet myself.

Uncle Grey's wreck of a house didn't have a shower, but it *did* have hot water and a bath. Okay, the hot water only arrived in the bath after the pipes sounded like they were trying to escape through the walls, but it did eventually arrive.

I filled the bath to the brim and got in.

"Ow!" I said, and leaped out of the bathtub. I'd forgotten that bruised shins and hot water don't mix.

Eventually, though, I climbed into the tub and settled back for some Serious Thinking. If I was going to survive sixty more days in the Beverly Hills Maximum-Security Prison—I mean, Beverly Hills Preparatory School for Very Snobby People—I was going to have to get creative, and fast. I needed a plan.

I needed protection. I didn't think I could stand another egging.

The steam rose from the surface of the water and drifted over toward the framed vintage movie posters that covered one wall. They were all from, like, a million years ago: 1940 or 1950 or something. *Old*. Maybe they reminded Uncle Grey of being young. Who knew? Who cared?

The important point is that one of them caught my eye.

I scraped the last piece of egg off my ear and smiled. The jackhammers stopped on the freeway construction site, and for the first time since I'd arrived back from BHP, 322 Chestnut Drive fell silent.

I stepped out of the bath (which had turned into a kind of disgusting egg-and-cement soup) and got dressed in some nonregulation clothes.

I had a plan.

I'm not saying it was the best plan anyone had ever come up with—or even the best plan *I* had ever come up with—but it was definitely A Plan and that was good enough for me right now.

CHAPTER 17

NO GHOSTS, NO SKELETONS

After a delicious dinner of murders and flies (see previous chapter), I got busy at the computer and designed what I needed in about an hour. It wasn't hard—just a couple of logos and some words on one sheet of paper. I wrote a few names on the back with question marks next to them, then put the sheet of paper down on some dusty floorboards and rubbed it backward and forward a few times. I scrunched the sheet up into a ball before carefully unscrunching it again and folding it in four. For this to work, this thing had to look legit. I put it in a book in my backpack and left it until morning.

Mom and Georgia both seemed to have settled into Beverly Hills without ANY problems. Like,

NONE. Georgia came back from her first day in the south wing of BHP, babbling about all the friends she'd made.

Okay, that was an exaggeration...but not by much. Clearly, it was only RAFE Khatchadorian in the Khatchadorian household who'd been singled out for special treatment by the Velociraptor, Mr. Fitzpatrick and his pet mustache, Egg Girl, Captain Shiny Hair, and the rest of the Winners Club.

Leaving Mom and Georgia watching TV, I spent the rest of that evening exploring the house.

Like I said earlier, Uncle Grey's place was full of junk. Or, possibly, stuff that just *looked like* junk. For all I knew, it had been worth a fortune at one time.

Say, sometime around 1889. Now it was mostly junk. At the very top of the house I found a set of stairs leading up to the attic. I know what you're thinking: *He's going to go up there and find a spooky secret. Maybe a ghost or two. Or the skeleton of some forgotten plumber.*

And you'd be wrong. What I found up there was WAAAY cooler than ghosts or skeletons.

I found Uncle Grey's art studio.

It had everything an artist could possibly need—great big skylights letting in, um, light; boxes of paints; stacks of blank canvases; easels; brushes; palettes; paper; pencils; masking tape; rags; turpentine; charcoal. You name it, it was all there on the paint-spattered floorboards. The walls were covered in sketches and paintings. All of them looked like they'd been done by Uncle Grey. There was that same messy blobbiness, that spidery line work, that sense of fun. Okay, everything was totally covered in dust and cobwebs so thick I would probably have needed a chain saw to cut through them, but to me, it was a treasure trove.

In the middle of the room was a huge canvas under a white sheet—the only protected item in the studio. I just *knew* that under that mysterious sheet lay Uncle Grey's masterpiece. I had a sudden image of me lifting the sheet to reveal a painting so flat-out AMAZING that art galleries all over the world would be throwing money at me...if I was willing to sell.

I flung off the sheet and saw...absolutely nothing. The canvas was blank.

CHAPTER 18

BRING ON THE DANCING UNICORNS

After the disappointment of the blank canvas in the attic, I went to bed, slept like a log—I never understood that saying. Do logs even sleep? No, I didn't think so—and woke up ready to face another day. Above my head, the jackhammers were silent and, through the dusty windows, I could see it was another gloriously sunny morning. That day at BHP was *fantastic*.

I made a bunch of great new friends and we spent the whole day eating cotton candy while dancing with unicorns across a glittering rainbow.

Ha! I just put that stuff in to see if you were paying attention, and it looks like some of you weren't.

So, there were (obviously) absolutely ZERO dancing unicorns, no rainbows, not a sniff of cotton candy, and definitely no new friends at Beverly Hills Maximum-Security Prison when I went back. That's not how life works. Not *my* life, anyway.

No, the way Rafe Khatchadorian's life works is more like this: day two at Beverly Hills Preparatory School for Very Snobby People started pretty much like day one. I didn't get tripped by

Cory Tadpole-Blurt, but I did get two uniform demerits from Mr. Fitzpatrick and one language demerit from a passing tree frog teacher. (Just to make it clear, he wasn't *teaching* tree frogs. I didn't know his name. He had a face like a tree frog.)

But I made it to recess without adding anything more to Demerit Mountain. At this rate, I wouldn't need to put the Plan into action.

How wrong I was.

After lunch, I was heading toward my locker when I noticed Cory Topknot-Beanhead lurking nearby with a creepy smirk plastered all over his shiny face.

I'm no Sherlock Holmes, but I knew this dude was up to something…and that something would probably not end well for me. I made a note to be on the lookout for Cory and the rest of the annoying Winners Club. I got to my locker, relieved to have made it past Toady-Bore without more trouble.

I heaved a stack of new textbooks out of my bag (I was the New Kid, remember, and every teacher had handed me enough books to buckle the knees of a bodybuilder). Keeping one eye on my enemies, I opened my locker door and was full-on *attacked* by a spider.

Yep, you heard me, a spider.

And not just your standard-issue spider, either. This was a great big, full-on horror-movie tarantula, which launched at me like I was fresh meat.

To say I was surprised would be putting it mildly.

Having a MASSIVE HAIRY SPIDER leap at your face ranks right up there (or down there, more accurately) with discovering you're standing on the back of a giant crocodile, and getting pranked by the biggest bully at summer camp—both of which had happened to me.

If I *had* to choose, I'd put the MASSIVE HAIRY SPIDER at the top of that list of terrible experiences. My screams could be heard on Mars.

Especially as the MASSIVE HAIRY SPIDER crawled up to my hair. For about twenty seconds, I twitched and shook like a—well, like a dude with a MASSIVE HAIRY SPIDER caught in his hair.

Eventually, the disgusting thing fell to the floor and went skittering away. I love most animals, but when it comes to spiders? I'm all for mass extermination.

I sat up, dazed—had I mentioned I was on the floor?—and looked at the sea of laughing faces.

For the second day in a row, I was the laughingstock of the school.

Cory Templeton-Bishbosh was nearby with his flock of cronies.

I looked at him and he looked at me. This meant war.

CHAPTER 19

THE DINOSAUR APPROACHES

Now, I had no proof that Captain Shiny Hair had anything to do with putting the MASSIVE HAIRY SPIDER in my locker, but I didn't *need* proof. I *knew* that creep had done it, and what's more, he knew *I* knew he'd done it. You following?

I was about to tell him exactly where to stick it when I saw the Velociraptor approaching, his nose twitching at the scent of trouble.

As soon as Cory spotted Principal Winton, he rushed over and started helping me to my feet. He changed his facial expression from "evil bully" to "concerned friend" in about 0.0006 of a second.

"What on earth is going on here?" the Velociraptor hissed. He bit the head off a nearby sixth grader and looked at me with his reptilian eyes while he munched.

"There was a spider in Rafe's locker, Principal Winton, sir," Cory said. For a moment I thought Captain Shiny Hair was going to add "Your Highness."

"A spider?" the Velociraptor said.

"Yes, sir. Quite a big one."

BIG? That thing needed its own atmosphere.

"You had a spider in your locker?" the Velociraptor said.

"But—but—someone put it there!" I sputtered.

As soon as the words were out of my mouth, I knew I'd made a mistake.

The Velociraptor leaned back, lifted his claws, and gave a kind of screech. "Three demerits!"

I thought he was signaling for the rest of the raptors, but when I saw Mr. Fitzpatrick snicker, I realized Principal Winton was *laughing*.

"One for illegal storage of an arachnid on school property, one for insolence in talking back to an adult, and one for no use of 'sir'!"

"Burn the witch!" Mr. Fitzpatrick yelled, his eyes glittering and his mustache vibrating like an angry caterpillar, although (now that I think about it) he probably didn't actually say "Burn the witch" out loud. Even BHP wouldn't allow the public burning of students...Would they? But he *looked* like he wanted to say it.

I was about to argue back when...a light bulb went on in my head. Arguing would get me exactly nowhere. Arguing with the Velociraptor would only land me in more trouble and let Cory Tartar-Buttface win.

I flashed back to the cunning plan I'd put together last night.

Be smart, whispered a voice in my head.

"It won't happen again, Principal Ve—Principal *Winton*, sir," I promised. "There'll be no more spiders in my locker. And I'll do my best to improve my school manners, sir."

"Six demeri—Oh." Principal Winton stopped midscream. "Oh, right. Yes, I see."

"And I'd like to put forward Cory for a School Spirit Award, if I may, Your Sirship," I said.

I had no idea if there was such a thing as a School Spirit Award, but I was guessing BHP would be *exactly* the kind of joint that would have one. I knew it had school spirit because I'd been given a demerit for not having any. "Cory was the first one to check to see if I was okay while everyone else was laughing. It wouldn't be fair if that went unrewarded, Lord Volde—Principal Winton."

Cory looked at me, puzzled. I was betting this wasn't going the way he thought it would go.

"Y-ess," Principal Winton said. He scratched his chin thoughtfully with one of his razor-sharp claws. It's hard to fool a velociraptor. Principal Winton knew there was something fishy going on, but he couldn't *quite* place his talon on it. "I suppose a School Spirit Award might be appropriate."

See? I was right.

The Velociraptor and Mr. Fitzpatrick scuttled back to their lair, and everyone else began drifting away.

"Thanks, buddy," I said to Cory, and walked away, lifting a book out of my bag and taking care to drop the sheet of paper I'd prepared last night.

Out of the corner of my eye, I saw Cory dart forward and pick it up. If I'd read this dude right, there was no way he'd tell me I'd dropped something. I kept walking and Cory didn't say a word.

Step One of the Plan was in action.

CHAPTER 20

NOWHERE TO RUN

I didn't get into any more trouble that day. That was a good thing.

On the other hand, there was nothing exactly pleasurable, either. I mean, I wasn't expecting *fun* or anything—this was still school, after all—but I'd kinda hoped I'd meet at least one sorta kinda somewhat cool kid. Big Red, who I'd assumed would become my buddy, ditched me about ten minutes after the spider incident. "I can't have the Winners Club thinking we're friends," he'd said.

So, at the end of another day, I was walking across the fields toward the back gates when I saw something terrible heading my way.

Egg Girl.

She was wearing decorated roller skates and sunglasses and a school uniform that definitely wasn't the BHP fancy dress. Egg Girl's uniform was kind of messy: just shorts, T-shirt, and baseball cap. She had a book bag slung over her shoulder and a set of headphones over her ears. If she'd been a BHP student, she'd have made my Demerit Mountain seem like a bump in the road.

I scanned the surroundings for somewhere to hide. (What do you mean "coward"? I'd been traumatized by my encounter with the MASSIVE spider, okay?) My shins began to throb. I didn't think they could take another kick. But there was nowhere to go and I was locked in Egg Girl's tractor beam.

CHAPTER 21

EGG GIRL MEET SOCKS

Egg Girl zipped down the slope at about the same speed as a Japanese bullet train (198 miles an hour, if you must know) and showed no sign of stopping.

Maybe that was her plan—to simply steamroll me on the BHP school drive and head for the hills.

She was still traveling at full speed when she got to within about two feet of me.

"Don't mash me!" I yelped, and clenched my butt.

Instead, Egg Girl zipped around me in a tight circle and skidded gracefully to a stop without so much as touching me.

My butt began to unclench. I eyed Egg Girl's feet.

"I'm not going to kick you, if that's what you're thinking," she said as she hung her headphones around her neck.

"N-no," I replied. "I was, um, just admiring your roller skates."

"Hand-painted AeroGlide 1480s with rebored Glissande trolleys," Egg Girl said. "Swedish-made carbon axles. Tungsten-reinforced chassis and an embedded performance-feedback microchip."

I blinked. Egg Girl knew a lot more than me about roller skates, which, considering all I knew was that they had wheels, wasn't saying much.

"Okay," I said.

She put out a hand. "Kasey Moran. Sorry."

"You're sorry for being called Kasey Moran?"

I was confused. I mean, my name is a bit of a mouthful but I'm not sorry about it.

Egg Girl punched me in the arm. It wasn't as bad as her shin kicks but it was still painful.

"Ow!" I yelped. "Will you *quit* kicking and punching me?"

"That's my name, you doofus. The 'sorry' was for yesterday." She pointed at my shins. "For the, uh, kicking and the egg stuff. I found out it wasn't you who egged our house."

"You live at BHP? I thought that was the caretaker's house?"

Kasey rolled her eyes and pointed a thumb at herself. "Yeah, my dad's the caretaker?" She stepped forward and rapped her knuckles on my forehead. "Hello? Anyone home? Jeez."

"Ow!" I danced back a few steps, out of range of Kasey and her knuckles. This was the most painful apology I'd ever received. It may have been the ONLY apology I'd ever received. I couldn't think of anything to say so I just kind of stood there like a dummy.

"All you rich kids are the same," Kasey said dismissively. "You meet an ordinary person and you don't know what to say." She started to skate off.

"Wait," I said. "I'm not rich!"

She cocked her head to one side. "So what are you doing at BHP?"

"It's a long story—a boring one."

Kasey smiled. "I'll be the judge of that." She nodded in the direction of her house. "Let's go, Socks."

"Socks?"

Kasey pointed at my starched BHP socks.

"Actually, the name's Rafe," I said.

"I think I'll stick with Socks," Kasey replied as she began doing backward figure eights toward her house.

CHAPTER 22

OLEG DULIATNEV

Yeah, I know.

You're thinking, *Hey, Rafe, this stuff about roller-skating Kasey is all well and good, but what was on that sheet of paper you dropped back near the lockers? You just left us hanging, dude! Fess up!*

Okay, I'll fess.

Let's park my friendship with Kasey over here and rewind to the sheet of paper. This is what it looked like:

Dear Mr. Khatchadorian,

This is the second time I have had to warn
you about breaking the rules of the Witness
Protection Program. As you know, your mixed-
martial-arts expertise makes you incredibly
dangerous. When I placed you at your last
school, I did not expect you to draw attention
to yourself by injuring quite so many bullies.
The FBI cannot continue paying hospital bills
because someone looked at you funny. As an ex–
Special Forces operative with links to the Mafia,
you have many skills, which, if used unwisely,
could result in much worse happening to those
who cross your path. We do not want to have to
take you out of Beverly Hills Preparatory School
because of some "unfortunate" incident—
like what happened last year in Philadelphia.

Regardless of any information you have, you
must control your tendencies.

The next scheduled assessment will take place
in three months. As always, burn this letter after
reading.

Senior Field Agent Scott Thurlow
Department of Witness Protection
FBI Office
32405 32nd Street, New York

Too much?
Not believable? Obviously fake? I didn't care.
If this dumb letter stopped Cory Tamworth-
Blythe from harassing me for five minutes, it would
be worth it. If he *did* believe my fake FBI letter,
then I also knew that the news would be all over
BHP faster than a dose of the flu. "Back off" would
be the message to the other BHP inmates, and I
could breeze through the next couple of months
without worrying about spiders in my locker, or
anything else the Winners Club had planned for me.
It was worth a shot.

CHAPTER 23

ALL ABOUT KASEY MORAN

Meeting Kasey made a difference to being at BHP. I hung out with her most days after school (bringing a change of clothes so I could get out of those socks *FAST*) and found out a few things about her.

She really liked roller skating. Not only did she roller-skate to and from school, she was a member of the LA Spitballers Roller Derby Team, along with Ms. Bennett, who was the only teacher at BHP who didn't seem to eat kids for lunch, according to Kasey.

Kasey was, like me, big on art. In her case, it mainly revolved around decorating her skates and the skates of the rest of the team. She was good at it, too.

She had lived in her house on the school grounds ever since she'd been born, which meant she knew more about BHP than anyone else (with, maybe, the exception of her dad).

Best of all, she introduced me to the Big Spaghetti Blob and Franco Bonini.

CHAPTER 24

THE BIG SPAGHETTI BLOB

Yyou've never seen the Big Spaghetti Blob? It's a Bonini!"

I shook my head for the third time. No matter how many times I shook it, Kasey couldn't believe it.

"But it's right there in the Great Hall, up above the stage where the school assembly is! You can't miss it! It's a Bonini!"

"Look," I said. "Just show me. It'll be easier. And stop saying 'It's a Bonini.'"

One of the advantages of being the daughter of the caretaker was that Kasey could get into BHP after everyone had left. Making sure her dad was safely in another part of the school, Kasey snuck us into the Great Hall. It was Friday evening, so there wasn't even a chance of bumping into one of the velociraptors. They were all at home, trying to forget about BHP until Monday morning.

The only times I'd been in the Great Hall were during the school assembly. I'd never seen the place without it being stuffed to the walls with kids and velociraptors. Now, even though it was still light outside, it seemed slightly spooky. Our footsteps echoed on the wooden floor. The place smelled of polish and the crushed dreams of children.

(Just kidding! It didn't smell of polish.)

Kasey walked to the middle of the room and stood there, looking at a white shape on the wall. "I don't believe it," she said. "He *did* it."

"Who? Did what?" I asked.

Kasey pointed at the white shape. "That's the Big Spaghetti Blob."

I cocked my head to one side. "Is it modern art? Some kind of minimalist thing?"

It looked like a plain old white sheet to me.

Kasey disappeared behind the stage and came out wheeling an enormous stepladder.

She pushed it into place below the white shape and started climbing.

"Winton has always hated the Big Spaghetti Blob," Kasey said. She got to the top and reached for what I could now see was a giant sheet. "Too *messy* for him, too *wild*. He's been threatening to cover it up for ages, but I never thought he'd do it after the school board wouldn't let him. Not when they use it in all the shiny brochures and everything. And not to something so…" Kasey stopped midsentence as she struggled with the sheet.

"Something so…?" I was desperate to see this thing now.

"So amazing!" Kasey said, giving the sheet a sharp tug.

I took a few steps back to get a better look.

"*That's* a Bonini," Kasey said.

← Mind being blown

CHAPTER 25

SEEING COLOR

It was a painting.

A gigantic, amazing, incredible, stupendous, sprawly MESS of a painting.

It was splotchy. It was wobbly. It was blue and black and green and yellow and orange and a few colors I didn't even recognize. Paint flew everywhere, and there were, I dunno, *things* hidden in the paint—sort of "realistic" objects, some animal shapes. Plants, maybe. It was impossible to tell, impossible to pin down.

I loved it.

And yes, it did look like a blob of spaghetti.

Kasey stepped off the ladder and stood next to me. "Not too shabby, eh?" she said, nudging me (painfully) in the ribs. She pointed at the painting.

"*Composition in Color* by Franco Bonini," she said.

I looked at the painting more closely. "This Franco Bonini, is he famous?"

Kasey nodded. "Massive. His paintings are in a museum. We can go see some tomorrow, if you like?"

"That'd be cool." I didn't say anything else because I was thinking of something. "And this painting would be worth, like, a ton of money?"

"Loads. *Millions*. The Tamworth-Blythes gave it to the school years ago."

"No wonder they walk around like they own the place," I said.

"They practically do," Kasey said. "They own almost everything else in Beverly Hills."

"Uh-huh," I said, only half listening.

There was something about *Composition in Color* that was giving me a weird little tickle somewhere in my brain.

I didn't know exactly what the tickle was telling me—assuming tickles can tell you anything—but I knew one thing: it looked an awful lot like the paintings back at 322 Chestnut Drive.

CHAPTER 26

PAINT ME

Just so you know, Mom and Georgia were still both doing fine. Georgia was loving school, blah-blah-blah, and Mom was getting awfully comfortable living in such a fancy neighborhood.

After dinner that Friday, she left me watching Georgia to "get a steam" at the spa, whatever that means, so I went straight up to the attic, leaving Georgia watching TV.

The big blank canvas was still there.

I looked at it, and it stared blankly back at me. "Paint me," it whispered.

I mean, it didn't actually speak or anything.

It wasn't haunted, or at least I don't think it was. That's just how it felt. Like it was talking. Or like Uncle Grey was talking to me (which, I admit, is kinda spooky).

"Paaaaaaint meeeeeee," whispered the canvas.

I thought about seeing the Bonini at BHP, and I let my eyeballs wander around the attic at Uncle Grey's paintings and drawings. They looked a lot like the painting at school. Which was a good thing…right? I still had that weird tickle, but I decided to think about what that could mean later. Right now, the canvas was talking.

"Come on, bud, we ain't got all day."

I picked up a paintbrush—a real fat one that sat nicely in my hand. It felt *good*, as though it belonged there. At the metal sink in one corner, I poured some water into an empty plastic bucket, grabbed a tube of paint—ocher, since you ask—and mixed the paint with the water. I stood in front of the canvas for a few seconds, waiting. I don't know what for, exactly. Inspiration? The return of my mojo? But then I plunged the brush into the water, drew back my painting arm, and dragged the brush across the white canvas in a messy, super-splashy, blobby, orangey-brown circle.

It felt great.

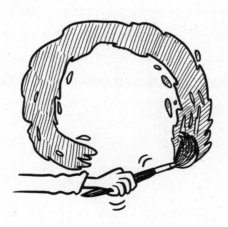

CHAPTER 27

TOTALLY EMBARRASSING DOOFUSES

The next day, Kasey came by to take me into the city. We were going to see the Boninis at the museum before heading to Golden Blades Stadium, where Kasey and the rest of the Spitballers were having a practice session. I couldn't wait. I'd never been to a roller derby.

By the way, this wasn't a date or anything icky like that. Just thought I'd make that clear.

A couple of buddies hanging out on a Saturday,
nothing to see here, nothing to get excited about,
move right along...

I was still emailing with Penelope every week. She'd give me updates about the latest animal they were saving, and I'd tell her all about becoming the most popular kid at BHP.

(Wishful thinking.)

Going to the museum with Kasey was a *NON-date*.

Which, of course, didn't stop Mom and Georgia from acting like a couple of TOTALLY EMBARRASSING DOOFUSES when Kasey arrived.

"Cool house," she said, skating inside. "Funky."

Mom gave me a wink that was supposed to be secret but wasn't. It was such an obvious wink that the draft from her eyelid knocked me off my feet.

CAPTAIN OBVIOUS

Georgia was even more obvious. "Is this your girlfriend, Rafe?" she said. "Oooooooooh!"

I was about to protest when Kasey beat me to it. "No," she said, all cool. "Socks and me are friends."

"Socks?" Georgia asked.

Kasey pointed to me. "That's what I call him." She raised her eyebrows in a question. "Because of the socks he has to wear."

"Oh yes," Georgia said. "So is that *friends* friends, or *boy and girl* friends?" My sister isn't someone who is put off easily.

"Friends friends," Kasey said. She skated expertly around the kitchen table and headed for the door. "Socks is my pal. Nothing else, okay?"

"Yeah," I said. "So—*thrrrrp* to you, Georgia." That *thrrrrp* was me blowing a raspberry, which may not have been the coolest thing I've ever done.

We battled across the garden and set off down the hill toward the city.

Next stop: the museum!

CHAPTER 28

IT'S A JELLYFISH

To get to the museum, Kasey took me on a kind of super-speed Beverly Hills tour. She was on her skates and I'd taken my skateboard, so we could move pretty fast, although we had to ignore dirty looks from people driving shiny cars. At least the roads were much smoother here than in Hills Village; no rocks to jump over or potholes to avoid.

Kasey pointed out the fancy stores, the country club. I'd worked at a fancy country club before, but this one was way bigger. As for the homes, I could barely see any because they were all hidden by these big gates that screamed *Stay Out*.

Eventually, we got to the museum.

Inside, we put our stuff in the coat check (after Kasey argued with a security guard about being able to keep her roller skates on—she lost) and headed to the Boninis.

"It looks like a jellyfish," I said. Kasey glared at me.

"That's a good thing!" I said, holding up my hands. "I like jellyfish!" (To be honest, I really don't.)

We were in front of a painting called *Ocean* by Franco Bonini. It was only the second one I'd ever seen after the Big Spaghetti Blob back in the Great Hall at BHP, but it was enough for me to know I was definitely a fan.

Ocean was big—about thirty-three square feet—mostly blue and green and white, and no matter what Kasey thought, it did look like a jellyfish. A kind of fat blue-green shape sat over to one side with lots of trailing "tentacles" drifting down and across. The more you looked at it, the more you kept thinking you could see *things* in there, like the ocean, fish, buildings, and fields. The trouble was, when you zoomed in, the squiggles weren't actually things at all...if you get what I mean.

Do you get what I mean? It's difficult to describe paintings, especially abstract paintings like *Ocean*.

CHAPTER 29

TICKLE, TICKLE

Just like the Big Spaghetti Blob at BHP, *Ocean* reminded me of every painting at 322 Chestnut Drive. That weird tickle was getting more ticklish. Could there be something fishy going on, and not just in the painting? Or was Uncle Grey just a really big Bonini fan?

"Painted in 1963," Kasey said, peering at the little label off to one side of the painting.

We carried on through the exhibition. It was like dipping your eyeballs in sunshine and candy. Or maybe it was more like being in an aquarium. Or a carnival for your brain.

We looked at drawings of lakes and giraffes and birds and swimming elephants and wrinkly old dudes and they were *all* fantastic.

I hadn't really realized until then that painting could be *fun* as well as, y'know, "serious" and "brainy" and all the other stuff it's supposed to be. By the time we'd reached the end of the exhibition, I wanted to race back to 322 Chestnut Drive and continue painting up in the attic.

But painting would have to wait, because I had my first visit to Golden Blades Stadium.

The stadium was in a totally different part of the city, so we got a bus that rattled west until Kasey jerked a thumb. "This is us."

The run-down industrial area where we got off seemed a million miles away from all the glitz of Beverly Hills. Kasey pointed at a dirty, white square building in the middle of a strangely glittering parking lot that was surrounded by a buckled and broken wire fence. A rusty metal sign missing a few letters and leaning at an angle stood at the entrance.

"This is the place," Kasey said, and skated off. "C'mon, I'm late!"

When I got closer, I saw that the parking lot was glittering because of all the broken glass scattered around. It looked like a bottle-breaking convention had been held there. Weeds poked through cracks in the cement, and black tire marks looped in figure eights across the whole place.

"Hooligans," Kasey muttered. "They come here at night and skid around in their cars and throw bottles out the window."

"Doesn't that damage their tires?"

Kasey gave a hard laugh. "They're not exactly Einsteins, Socks." She slid to a halt next to the entrance to the stadium. "It's great, huh?"

I nodded. "It's, um, got character."

FYI, "It's got character" is code for "This place needs knocking down."

Close up, Golden Blades Stadium looked terrible.

Big chunks of broken brick, gaping holes, shattered glass, patched-up windows—you get the picture.

"The lease on this place runs out in a couple of months," Kasey said. "If we don't raise some serious funds to renew the lease, we're gonna be homeless. They're putting a freeway right across here."

I made a sympathetic face. What else could I do? "And you know what makes it worse? Every time I see Cory Tamworth-Blythe around BHP, it reminds me."

"What's he got to do with it?"

"His dad owns the company that's putting in the freeway. TB Construction. Tamworth-Blythe Construction."

Just when I thought it was impossible to hate Cory Tincan-Buttockface any more than I already did, something would pop up to take it to another level.

LOLA THE ROLLER
AND DEE STROYER

While both of us thought about creative ways we'd like to see Tincan-Buttockface suffer, we scooted across to the stadium entrance.

Outside, there were six or seven cars parked in the shade of a rickety-looking tin roof that ran the length of one wall, along with a monster truck with tires that reached my shoulder, two motorbikes, and a couple of bicycles. Muffled shouts and bangs echoed from somewhere inside. A whistle blew.

"C'mon!" Kasey said. "They've started!"

We scuttled through the entrance and into the concrete guts of the stadium. Kasey ran up a flight of steps with me right behind, and I got my first glimpse of a roller derby.

While Golden Blades Stadium wouldn't win any prizes for beauty, it sure looked like it meant business. The stadium was basically a big hall. On four sides were rows of grandstand seats facing an oval wooden track—the kind you see in Olympic cycling events. (I found out later that that was exactly what it was, except the LA Spitballers had taken it over for roller skating.) A bunch of girls and women were skating around and around.

They all wore helmets and knee and elbow pads and looked tough.

The Spitballers!

The Mean Machine   Miss Creant   Dee Stroyer (Ms. Bennett)   Kiki   Lola the Roller

"Hey, Kase!" one of the skaters shouted. "Nice of our star jammer to show up!"

"Sorry!" Kasey shouted as she put on her helmet and fastened her pads. She slid smoothly onto the track and bumped fists with a couple of the skaters. One of them looked up at me and waved. I looked closer and, as I waved back, saw it was Ms. Bennett. She looked waaay different.

The only other person who wasn't playing was a guy with a beard sitting way up in the stands. I figured he also knew someone from the team. Finding a seat, I took my sketchbook out of my backpack and settled in to find out exactly what roller derby was all about.

After ten minutes, I'd figured it out. Roller derby was fighting on skates.

CHAPTER 31

MONDAY

A roar that turned my guts to mush thundered from behind the iron bars of the gate guarding the entrance to the Colosseum. It ricocheted around the stadium and the bloodthirsty crowd screamed back.

RAAAAAAAAAAAAAOOOOOOOAAAWW-WOOOOOARGH!

If I hadn't been tied to a stake in the center of the arena, I'd have dropped to my knees. Instead, I watched in trembling horror as two muscle-bound guards (who looked A LOT like Miller the Killer, now that I come to think about it) heaved back the iron gates and bolted for safety.

For a few seconds, nothing happened. Everyone inside the Colosseum (but especially me) gazed at the unprotected black tunnel and held their breath.

RAAAAAAAAAAAAAAOOOOOOOAAAWW-WOOOOOARGH!

And now the beast came thudding in and we could see the five-headed creature clearly in every horrific detail: the drooling mouths filled with razor-sharp teeth; the pitiless, deep-set, totally uncaring eyes of a school principal; the huge scaly tail whipping from side to side; and (perhaps worst of all) the leather-bound student handbook strapped to its pockmarked back.

"Please, no!" I moaned. "Anything but *that!*"

The creature stepped forward, growling and drooling. It put the biggest and ugliest of its faces close to mine. I tried to pull away but couldn't.

My nostrils filled with the creature's foul breath, and I glimpsed the remains of other poor souls who'd been wedged in between its canines. The creature stood upright, threw back its heads, and roared once again, this time louder and wilder than before.

RAAAAAAAAAAAAAOOOOOOAAAWW-WOOOOOARGH!

The crowd fell silent as the noise faded, and in that silence, I heard a small child's voice. "What is that horrible thing, Daddy? I'm scared!"

I twisted around and saw a man holding an infant close to his chest.

"That?" the man said in an awed whisper that carried clear across the arena. He extended a finger at the creature. "That's...that's *Monday*, son."

CHAPTER 32

WHAT'S A LACROSSE?

Okay, maybe that was a bit overdramatic, but that didn't stop me from crying real tears on Monday.

The weekend was officially *over*, it was raining heavily (of course it was), and I had to survive another Kasey-less week at Beverly Hills Maximum-Security Prison. I didn't have high hopes. Although that last chapter in the Colosseum was obviously all in my head, the harsh reality at BHP wasn't much better.

The day began with my usual collection of demerits from my teachers. A language demerit here, a uniform demerit there. I was beginning to think of demerits as small furry animals for some reason. I mean, there must have been someone somewhere keeping score of all these demerits, but so far I couldn't see what they were *for*.

Anyway, after getting the demerits, I turned up for the first lesson of the day.

Lacrosse.

Okay, here's the thing. I didn't know what a lacrosse was. Now I do. And I can tell you this:

I never want to play it again, if that's all right with you. Like, NEVER—NEVER, NEVER, NEVER.

Is that enough nevers? *NEVER*.

BHP kids play a lot of sports. As those of you who have been reading all my books will know, sports are not something I'm good at. I mean, there was that one *freaky* time back at my old middle school when I semi-accidentally became halfway good at football, but that lasted about eleven seconds.

It's not that I don't *want* to be good at sports. I *do*.

People who are good at sports are usually popular. They usually have an easier time at school than people like me. So I really wanted to do good lacrosse.

The eeny weeny teeny tiny problem was this: Have you seen the *size* of the kids who play lacrosse?

CHAPTER 33

BREAK A LEG

Go and stand out on the crease, Khatchadorian,"
Mr. Lafoulis, the gym teacher, said. "You're on
defense."

I tried to figure out what he was talking about.
I had no idea what a crease was. Pant crease? I
checked my gym shorts, but I couldn't find a crease.
I'd probably have gotten a demerit if I had.

"The crease?" Mr. Lafoulis said, as though
repeating the word would make me suddenly
understand. He looked at me again, held a hand
to his forehead, and muttered something in
French. (Mr. Lafoulis was actually French. It
wasn't like he was speaking French for some
weird reason.)

"By the goal?" I tried to answer, but when I did, all that came out was drool—thanks to my mouth guard. Mr. Lafoulis gave me two demerits for not answering properly.

A kid who was smaller than me and who was shaking like a leaf stopped me as I ran past. "You're new here, right?" he murmured, his eyes darting one way and then another.

I nodded.

"A word of advice," he said. "Get injured—as soon as you can. I mean, like a broken wrist/leg/ face kind of injury. Maybe lose an eye? Trust me, Lafoulis won't let you leave for anything less. It's the only way you're gonna survive."

"Oh-kay," I said, moving out of range. There was a wild look in the kid's eyes that I didn't like. Broken face? Lose an eye? How bad could lacrosse be? Between my chest protector, shoulder pads, and lacrosse gloves, I felt like the Bubble Boy.

And then I saw the kid heading right for me.

He looked about twenty-three years old. He had a beard and weighed three hundred pounds—*all* of it solid muscle. His name was Greg. I found this

out because Greg body-checked me so many times
that by the end of the first quarter, I couldn't even
feel my bones.

But I can tell you that I didn't break a single
one.

CHAPTER 34

SNEAKY BUSINESS

Tuesday wasn't much better.

That's it.

No—wait—there was something else worth
mentioning among all the other lousy stuff.

I was slouching past the Great Hall on the
way to class when I noticed the board displaying
the names of all the past class presidents of
BHP. There were more than 140 of them, and
I remembered what Mr. Ato had said back in
Hills Village about Uncle Grey having been one.
I worked out the years and followed the list of
names down toward 1958 and found...

Nothing.

There was no mention of a Khatchadorian
anywhere. See?

1956: Williams, S.
1957: Harper, D.
1958: Tamworth-Blythe, H.
1959: Mills, F.

I frowned. That was weird. Why would Uncle Grey pretend to have been class president? I mean, who was he trying to impress?

It was typical that there'd be a Tamworth-Blythe on there—it was probably Cory's grandfather—and typical that his name was shinier than the rest, too. Poor old Mills, F. and Harper, D. were faded in comparison. Close up, the wooden board was paler under *Tamworth-Blythe, H.*, too, as though a name had been scrubbed out and a new one painted over it. I moved to one side so that the light caught the board and there, hidden underneath *Tamworth-Blythe*, I could see the faint outlines of *Khatchadorian, G.*

Uncle Grey had been rubbed out. Literally.

CHAPTER 35

THE MYSTERY OF THE
DISAPPEARING NAME

Rubbed out!

It was an outrage! After all he'd done for the school, Khatchadorian, G. had been airbrushed from history!

I didn't actually *know* that Khatchadorian, G. had done anything for BHP...in fact, now that I came to think about it, I didn't know much about Uncle Grey, period. What? I never said I was a detective. Plus, there has been a ton of *really* difficult stuff I've had to do since arriving in Beverly Hills. Digging around some old relative's past hasn't exactly been high on my list of priorities. But that wasn't the point. He'd been given the role of class president and deserved to be remembered. There was definitely something fishy going on.

I was so wrapped up in the Mystery of the Disappearing Name that I didn't hear the *tik-tak* of claws on wood before it was too late.

"Loitering in the corridors, I see, Mr. Khatchadorian," a familiar reptilian voice hissed.

I whirled around to find myself face-to-face with Principal Winton and, as always, his faithful enforcer, Mr. Fitzpatrick, and his equally faithful mustache.

"Guilty, he is!" Mr. Fitzpatrick cackled. *"Eighteen thousand demerits!"* He lunged at me, snapping his jaws together. *"Twenty thousand demerits!"* The ends of his mustache whipped my face.

"Easy, Fitzie, easy," Principal Winton whispered, and Mr. Fitzpatrick pulled back, snarling. Principal Winton turned his hooded reptilian eyes toward the board and then back to me. "Was there something of interest you were looking for?"

That little warning bell sounded inside my head. "I was, er, admiring the lettering, sir," I said. "Very, um, good lettering, sir."

It wasn't exactly smooth, but it was the best I could do on short notice. Have you ever tried lying convincingly to a velociraptor? Didn't think so.

"A calligrapher, eh?" Principal Winton murmured.

"I enjoy painting, sir," I said. "Like my uncle." Principal Winton's eyes flashed. For a horrible, long moment I thought he was going to lean forward and bite my head clean off.

"Uncle?" he repeated.

I nodded. "My great-uncle Grey," I said. "He was a painter, Your Sirness. That's why I'm at BHP. Uncle Grey must have been very proud of BHP. Of course, he was here a long time ago, sir. Before you, I mean. And before Mr. Fitzpatrick. Basically, he was here before everyone. Sir."

I was babbling. I closed my mouth.

Principal Winton's eyes were now so hooded he looked as if he were asleep. "Khatchadorian—that's an unusual name," he said. "And I have an almost photographic memory. I think I would remember if someone with a name like that had been here before you." The Velociraptor drew closer and lowered his voice to a nasty whisper. "I don't believe your uncle was *ever* a student at BHP."

I knew enough to keep quiet. I didn't want my head bitten off. I liked my head. It was the only one I had. "Can I go, sir?" I asked. "I'm late for, um, lacrosse practice."

I was lying, of course, but help came from an unexpected direction.

"I LIKE LACROSSE!"

Mr. Fitzpatrick screamed so suddenly that both Principal Winton and I jumped. *"YES, I DO!"* He turned bright red and went back to chewing his mustache.

Principal Winton threw back his head and made that *click-clack* sound velociraptors make (the ones in the movies, anyway).

"So, I'll just go," I said, creeping toward the exit.

Once I'd reached the door, I looked back and saw Principal Winton hop up onto a nearby table, his claws held out in front of him, while Mr. Fitzpatrick gnawed on a chair leg.

BHP was one seriously messed-up school. Or, possibly, I was exaggerating again.

CHAPTER 36

BEAM ME UP

By Wednesday I figured my fake FBI letter had done the trick. My sneaky scheme must have worked, because Cory and the rest of the Winners Club hadn't so much as glanced my way since. So when I opened my locker and ANOTHER MASSIVE HAIRY SPIDER leaped straight onto my face, it was (to put it lightly) a big shock. It went something like this: I open the locker. Spider leaps onto face. I collapse onto floor. Cue uncontrollable laughter from everyone at BHP.

I lay on the ground, watching the spider crawl off into the distance.

A face came into view. Great.

"Oh, hey," I said. "My favorite bully."

"How are you feeling, *Oleg*?" Cory snickered. "Hope whoever put that spider inside your locker knows mixed martial arts. I wouldn't want you to *hurt* anyone."

I could hear the Winners Club laughing but didn't have the energy to respond. This was just like being back in Hills Village, except I was wearing starched socks, which meant—obviously— it was much, much worse.

CHAPTER 37

RAFE GETS HIS MOJO BACK

I'll spare you the horrors of what happened on Thursday and Friday. All you need to know is that the Winners Club was winning big when it came to doing battle with me.

SCORE

Winners Club **8**

Rafe **0**

On Friday night, with Georgia sleeping over at one of her HUGE number of new best friends' places (how did she *do* that?) and Mom getting another steam (she didn't say where she was going, but she practically leaped over me to get out), I spent as much time as I could in the attic at 322 Chestnut Drive. BHP was proving to be world-class when it came to bullying, but there was one way I could forget all about Cory and his minions.

Up in the attic, I painted and drew like I'd never done before.

Maybe I was mad. Maybe the ghost of Uncle Grey was working my arms. Who knows? All I *did* know was that my painter's block was well and truly over.

My mojo was back.

As the painting took shape, I had time to think about stuff. When it's going well, painting has that effect on me. I can sort of concentrate on the important things and block out all the other parts that just get in the way. While I was painting in the spirit of Uncle Grey, or maybe Franco Bonini, or both, I could see things clearly. And I decided I would:

1. See out my sentence at BHP so we could sell 322 Chestnut Drive and take our million bucks back to Hills Village, where

we'd live like emperors for the rest of our days. Or something like that.

2. Keep painting this painting.
3. Find out more about the Bonini paintings and figure out what the connection was between Franco Bonini and Uncle Grey. Had Uncle Grey really painted *Composition in Color*, or was I barking up the wrong tree and Bonini had definitely painted it AND some (or all) of the paintings at 322 Chestnut Drive?
4. Work out exactly why Uncle Grey's name had been scrubbed off the BHP board.
5. Keep being friends with Kasey aka Lola and her cool Spitballers for as long as I could.
6. Get revenge on Cory Tamworth-Blythe.
7. Become the first teenager to set foot on Saturn.

Aha! Gotcha! I only put that in to see if you were paying attention, and some of you weren't.

I blobbed a particularly blobby blob of deep blue paint onto the canvas and flicked my wrist to squodgle it around (yes, I know that's not an actual word). I'd managed to survive two weeks at BHP. I'd been attacked by a tarantula (twice), been given six trillion demerits, been publicly humiliated, had my shins kicked, and been turned into an omelet, BUT I had also met Kasey and the Spitballers and got my painting mojo back.

All things considered, it wasn't a bad deal.

CHAPTER 38

THE VOICE OF REASON

I'd been looking forward to hanging out with Kasey that weekend, so on Saturday morning I was a little surprised when she didn't call.

It wasn't like I had anyone else to talk to, so I finally decided to call her. And it turned out Kasey had much bigger things to worry about.

"I'm coming over," she said. "I need to get out of here."

"What happened?"

"I'll tell you when I get there."

Now Kasey was sitting up in the attic with me. Both of us were leaning back against the wall and looking at my painting.

"I like it," Kasey said. "I really like it."

"Never mind the painting. What's up?"

"I love the orange. The way it mixes with th—"

"Stop," I said, and shifted around to face her. "C'mon, what is it?"

"They're kicking us out," Kasey said, chewing her nails and looking like she wanted to strangle someone. Or kick 'em in the shins. Whichever was more painful.

"Who?"

"Yesterday, Principal Winton told Dad we'll

need to find somewhere else to live from next semester on. They're knocking down the house and turning it into a parking lot. Winton's getting a new office and he wants a bigger car space."

"He's knocking down your house to make a *parking lot*?" I couldn't believe it. "They can't do that, can they?"

Kasey nodded. "Dad says there's nothing we can do. He'll still work at the school, but we'll have to find a home somewhere else. Probably miles away, too. We can't afford to stay around here. I've lived at BHP all my life, Rafe. I don't want to move."

"Oh man." I put my arm around Kasey and we sat there, looking at the painting without saying anything for a while because there wasn't really anything to say.

Sometimes life sucks.

CHAPTER 39

MR. FROSTY PAYS A VISIT

Kasey had recovered a bit by midday, and we headed over to Golden Blades for her practice session. It looked like so much fun I wished I could play, but there were three reasons I couldn't:

1. I couldn't roller-skate;
2. the Spitballers were a women's team; and
3. I was too scared.

When we got there, the rest of the Spitballers were gathered in a tight knot over by one side of the track. In the middle was the guy with the beard I'd seen last week, the only other person, apart from me, not there for practice. As Kasey and

I got closer, I saw with a shock that the bearded guy was Frost DeAndrews!

Frost DeAndrews is a fancy-schmancy Australian art critic I met when I won a trip to Sydney, and who I'd accidentally involved in an unfortunate exploding toilet/rampaging zombie incident at Shark Bay. Despite that shark/zombie thing, Frost had liked my stuff, at one point comparing me to Wilhelm Van Purpleschpittel and the Contemporary Burble Movement—What? You haven't heard of them? Anyway, Frosty and I go way back. The big question was, what was a fancy Australian art critic doing at an LA Spitballers roller derby practice?

"Mr. Khatchadorian. Delighted to see you again," he said, in a not-particularly-delighted-to-see-you kind of voice. It didn't bother me. That's just the way old Frosty is. We shook hands.

"Frosty!" I said, patting him on the shoulder. "What are you doing here?"

"I could ask you the same question. Please remove your hand from my shoulder. And nobody calls me Frosty," he said frostily. *"Nobody."*

"I'll leave you two to catch up," Kasey said with

a wink, and skated off to join the practice session.

"So," I said, trying to recover, "why are you in America, at Golden Blades of all places, Fro—Mr. DeAndrews?"

"I'm visiting my sister," Frost DeAndrews replied. He waved a hand in the direction of the Spitballers. "She plays for them. Dee Stroyer."

My jaw dropped so low my chin bounced off the floor. *"Ms. Bennett?"* I said once I'd recovered. "She teaches at my school!"

"You're a BHP student?" Frost DeAndrews sounded surprised. Astonished, even. He raised an eyebrow. Just one.

I explained the whole Uncle Grey thing and Frost got excited. I could tell because he raised an eyebrow two millimeters when I got to the part about the Franco Bonini paintings, but otherwise he didn't react.

When I was finished, he pursed his lips and looked at me with roughly zero enthusiasm.

There was a silence that lasted about a year. I was beginning to remember how it was being around old Frosty. Eventually, just as I was considering making a run for it, he eyed the sketchbook I was carrying as if it were a dead fish.

"Your latest work?" he said, yawning.

I nodded, pleased he'd shown some interest. "I've been struggling for a while, to be honest, Mr. DeAndrews, but since I've started doing these Bonini-inspired drawings and paintings, things are getting better."

Frost sat down and stuck out a hand. "I rather think I'll be the judge of *that*," he sniffed.

I handed over the sketchbook and sat next to him like a prisoner waiting for his sentence.

CHAPTER 40

PAH!

Remarkable," Frost DeAndrews said. He closed my sketchbook and handed it back to me.

"Remarkable?" I said.

Remarkable was *good*. If someone as famous and knowledgeable as Frost DeAndrews thought my sketches were *remarkable*, I was doing the right thing and 322 Chestnut Drive was working its strange magic. I was over the artist's block, I was on the way back up, I could—

"It's remarkable that they can all skate so well," Frost DeAndrews said. "While they're fighting, I mean. Remarkable."

I looked at my sketchbook. "But what about my artwork?"

Frost DeAndrews wrinkled his nose. "Pah."

"Pah?" I repeated. I wasn't sure what "pah" meant, but it didn't sound promising. On the other hand, it didn't sound completely *terrible*, either.

Pah! I found the drawings to be largely derivative, faux-Pollock in nature, but the paintings contain traces of potential avenues of further perambulatory explanation. Although primarily pastiche, they contain echoes of American abstract expressionism filtered through the ho-hum assumed vortex of contemporary angst...

"So," I said uncertainly, "you like them?"

"Rather," Frost murmured, "they are precisely eighty-two-point-six percent more than passable." While I was still trying to work out what Frost meant, he leaned forward and tapped a bony finger on my sketchbook. "Listen,

Mr. Khatchadorian, Dee asked me here to advise the Spitballers about painting an artwork on the side of this ghastly ruin in an effort to supply some much-needed cheer and spruce the place up for the big fundraiser they're planning to hold in three weeks. How about you and your friend Kasey come up with something?"

"You want us to paint a mural?"

Frost DeAndrews tapped a knuckle on my forehead. "Hello? Anyone home? Of course I want you to paint a mural! That's why I was moving my lips and sounds were coming out of my mouth. I'll recommend to Dee that you and your friend should be the ones to decorate the stadium. Three weeks, remember. You'll have to get your skates on. Har har."

Frost got to his feet. He opened the sketchbook to a double page and pointed to a painting I'd done a couple of days after visiting the museum.

"Use this one as the basis for your design," he said. "And I'll come around to your place and see your uncle's paintings. Maybe there's something to your claims. My secretary will make the arrangements."

Frost DeAndrews turned, blew a kiss to his sister, and left.

I sat back, stunned, thinking about how big the outside of Golden Blades was. We were going to need plenty of paint.

CHAPTER 41

A BIG BLOBBY MESS

Ms. Bennett had listened to her brother, and the Spitballers had approved our design. During the art lessons at BHP, Ms. Bennett helped me map it out. Her lessons were just about the only thing at BHP I actually *liked*.

By Sunday night, the stadium wall had been transformed into a blank canvas by a team of Spitballers using white paint donated by a couple whose daughter skated for the team. They were also supplying the paint for the mural.

On Monday, Kasey and I sketched the main parts of the mural, and then we began painting. It was hard work, but I loved every single paint-spattered minute and I was pretty sure Kasey felt the same. More importantly, I think working on the

mural helped Kasey forget—for a while, at least—
about being booted out of their house. The weather
helped us, too, as if it were on our side. The whole
time we were painting, there wasn't a drop of rain.
When night fell, we continued to paint, using a
set of outdoor road construction lights we'd been
loaned by another Spitballer parent.

And the Spitballers themselves pitched in,
turning up in old clothes to splash and spray and
fling paint all over the old stadium. Big fingers of
paint slithered down the wall and onto the parking
lot, mingling in a giant multicolored, footprint-
patterned mess.

We could have put down sheets to keep the
mural on the wall, but we wanted the thing to ooze
off the edges, as if it were just having too much fun
to stay in one place. That was what Franco Bonini's
and Uncle Grey's paintings were like, and I wanted
this to be the same—a wobbly, wiggly, rebellious
blast of FUN and movement.

Of course, we got absolutely covered in paint
every time. It was messy, it was chaotic, it was
fantastic!

And, slowly, the Golden Blades mural took shape.

CHAPTER 42

WHEN THE SUN SHINES, EXPECT RAIN

The mural was going great. I was actually enjoying living in Beverly Hills. The Winners Club had stopped bullying me, for the most part. Kasey's dad had heard about a nice apartment they could move into next semester. Tickets for the Spitballers fundraiser were selling well. Mom and Georgia seemed to be having a good time, although I was worried about how Mom would settle back into our normal life in Hills Village, without shopping and steams and spas. My painting in the attic, although stopped in its tracks by the mural, was still going to be there when I'd finished. Frost DeAndrews had dropped by to look at Uncle Grey's paintings. He'd taken a bunch of photos, had made some notes, and had gone away after telling me he liked the painting in the attic. I told him about the tickle in my brain about *Composition in Color*, and about Franco Bonini and Uncle Grey, and which paintings were real Boninis and which weren't and how confusing it all was, and Frost told me he'd look into it.

So, like I said, things were going well for once.

I should have known it was too good to be true.

CHAPTER 43

SOCK INSPECTION

It's funny how things turn out.

How big changes can be started by tiny things, I mean. I guess if I hadn't had that extra piece of toast that Monday morning, if I had stopped to tie my shoelaces, if it had been raining and I'd taken the bus to BHP instead, none of what I'm about to tell you would have happened.

But I did eat the extra toast, I didn't tie my shoelaces, and it hadn't rained—all of which meant that I bumped into Mr. Fitzpatrick and Principal Winton at exactly 9:03 a.m. that Monday.

Mr. Fitzpatrick did his usual thing—slapping me with demerits for my starched socks not being starched enough.

"Those are practically sagging!" he barked. *"Three demerits!"*

"Tut, tut," Principal Winton tutted.

"I think they softened in the laundry, Your Sirships," I said, but Principal Winton wasn't finished. He was looking at me in a funny way. He cocked his head to one side and squinted.

"You've had a lot of demerits, haven't you, Khatchadorian?" he said.

Mr. Fitzpatrick, lurking at the principal's shoulder, sniggered. "*A lot!*" he squawked.

"One or two." I gulped. "Sir."

I didn't like the way this was going. It looked very much like I was about to find out exactly what those demerit points were for. And I was betting it was nothing good.

Principal Winton produced an electronic tablet from his jacket and jabbed a claw at the screen. "As I thought. You've passed the one-thousand mark, Mr. Khatchadorian. Remarkable for a mere four weeks at BHP."

I blushed. "Well, I don't want to brag, but—"

"This is not a laughing matter!" Principal Winton screeched. "One thousand demerits means death by tiger."

"What?!" I gasped.

"Yes," Principal Winton said, "you will be smeared with meat and placed in a pit, where you will be eaten by the school ti—"

Mr. Fitzpatrick leaned across Principal Winton and pointed to something on the screen. Both of them looked disappointed.

"Ah," Principal Winton said, "yes, thank you, Mr. Fitzpatrick." He turned back to me. "I seem to have made a small error, Khatchadorian. The *correct* punishment for one thousand demerits is not, it seems, death by tiger, but detention. You will be in *detention* after school every day this week for two hours."

I breathed a sigh of relief as they walked away. Death by tiger hadn't sounded good.

And then it hit me like a smack across the face with a wet fish. If I was in detention all week, I wouldn't be able to finish the mural at Golden Blades.

It was the last straw.

After everything that had happened lately, I'd had enough of Principal Winton and his stupid uniform rules and his stupid office expansion plan. It was time for Rafe Khatchadorian and Kasey Moran to take matters into their own hands.

I didn't stop to think about the consequences. Don't forget there was a million bucks riding on me staying at BHP. But did I think about that? Nope. All I knew right then was that we needed to take a stand.

It was time to strike back at the Evil Empire.

It was time to fight for freedom from sock inspections.

It was time to stand up to bullies and idiots who preferred parking lots to people.

In short, it was time for *revenge*.

CHAPTER 44

BITTEN BY THE REVENGE BUG

I had plenty of time to think about exactly what shape our revenge should take during that week's detention.

Detention was in the school library—as if going to the library were punishment!—directly opposite the swimming pool. This being BHP, the pool was more like something you'd see at the Olympics. It had everything: a fifty-meter competition pool, a twenty-five-meter lap pool, a diving pool, seating for about eighty thousand people, an electronic scoreboard, giant TVs...they probably had a water park stashed out back somewhere.

The lights were on inside the pool complex, and I could see the BHP swim team training. Needless to say, Cory Turtle-Burphole was on the team. I watched him adjust his goggles and dive effortlessly into the water. I watched Principal Winton walk up and down the side of the pool, shouting instructions through a megaphone and glancing frequently at a stopwatch in his hand.

The Velociraptor was a strict swim coach and never missed a session—or so I'd been told.

There he was, in a full tracksuit with a towel slung around his neck as if he'd actually been swimming. I guessed the team was getting ready for the big swim meet against BHP's biggest rival, Woodland Middle School, on Monday. I'd seen the posters around the school, and old Winton had droned on about the competition in assembly that morning. The whole school would be watching, and BHP, Principal Winton reminded us, had never lost to Woodland.

I was so busy thinking about how I could sneak up and push Principal Winton into the deep end that I didn't notice a creepy-crawly critter creepily crawling onto my arm until it was too late.

There was a line of fire ants leading out the window. Taking care not to get stung again, I followed the line to a small heap of dirt on the strip of grass outside. Looking up, I saw Principal Winton and—BINGO!—just like that, the whole plan came into my head, clear in every last detail.

CHAPTER 45

I LOVE IT

That's it? *That's* the great plan?" Kasey raised an eyebrow.

We were in her kitchen after I'd finished the last detention of the week. Revenge on Cory would have to wait. I wasn't that clever, so I was taking this one mission at a time.

The whole thing had sounded totally great in my head back in the library, but now I was feeling less sure. Kasey had come back from a session on the mural, and her hair was covered in paint. It was all still going okay, but without me there it had slowed down a lot. There was a chance we might not get it done in time for the fundraiser, which only made us even more mad at Principal Winton.

Anyway, where were we? Oh yes. Kasey's eyebrow wasn't sure about the plan.

"Uh-huh," I said, nodding. "That's the plan. Don't you like it?"

"No."

"Oh."

Kasey leaned forward and smiled. "I don't *like* it, I LOVE it!" She danced around and punched the air. "Oh man! This is going to be GREAT! What do we need? Let's get started!"

Kasey began opening cupboards and drawers, looking so eager I immediately began to have second thoughts. Were we going too far? What if I'd started something that would get out of control?

Kasey raised her hands in the air. She was holding a pair of thick rubber gloves, a plastic container with a lid, and a large spoon. "Let's go!"

CHAPTER 46

EIGHT HUNDRED ANTS, ONE BIG SPOON

I don't think it's giving too much away to tell you that the first component of my brilliant revenge plan involved collecting a bunch of fire ants. Kasey was going to handle the actual collecting.

She'd tried to give me some baloney about *me* doing the collecting, but I was having none of it.

"No way!" I protested. "Look at my hand!"

From that one fire ant bite, my hand had swollen to the size of a small lacrosse ball, which STILL wouldn't have been enough for me to get out of lacrosse.

Kasey and I were hiding behind a bush at the

back of BHP's library, roughly where I'd spotted the fire ants the day before.

"There," I said, pointing to the target.

Kasey pulled on the heavy-duty protective gloves and grabbed the spoon. "Get the container ready. Once these suckers realize what's going on, they'll be after us. We have to get in, get out, no hanging around!"

I nodded.

Kasey bent over the heap of dirt that marked the tip of Fire Ant Town. I crouched next to her with the open container.

"All good?" Kasey said. "Are we a go?"

I nodded. "Affirmative. Operation Fire Ant is a go." Kasey dug the spoon into the dirt. Immediately, a million angry fire ants swarmed out like an army of crazy zombies thirsty for blood.

"Get them!" I yelped as I watched the ants heading straight for my foot.

"Aw, gee, really?" Kasey said. "You think I should?" (She was being sarcastic, in case you were wondering.) Kasey scooped up about eight hundred ants and put her hand over the spoon. "Quick!" she snapped. "I can feel 'em biting!"

This had to be done right. One mistake and we'd be overrun by fire ants.

I dropped the lid.

"Run!" I yelled, but Kasey stopped me with an elbow to the ribs.

"Don't quit on me, soldier! Pick up that lid!"

I looked down at the writhing mass of fire ants. "Do it!" Kasey shouted. "I can't hold on much longer!"

I reached down and lifted the lid. Kasey emptied the spoonful of ants into the tub and I slammed on the lid.

"Mission accomplished!" Kasey yelled, and we bolted for freedom just as the first of the fire ant zombies reached our feet.

It had been close—too close—but stage one of my plan was a success.

CHAPTER 47

NO FIRE ANTS WERE HARMED DURING THE MAKING OF THIS BOOK

S tage two was easy. We took the tub of fire ants and put them in the freezer of Kasey's fridge. Freezing them wouldn't kill the ants, just slow them down for a while until they began to warm up. For this thing to work, there had to be a delay.

With the ants safely stowed, we were ready for Monday.

CHAPTER 48

WHAT COULD POSSIBLY GO WRONG?

I hadn't realized what a big deal the BHP-vs.-Woodland swimming match would be.

The event was due to start at midday, with the final race—the relay—happening around three o'clock. People started arriving at eleven, and by eleven thirty the parking lot was overflowing.

"This place could do with more parking spaces," I said.

Kasey kicked me in the shins. I probably deserved it.

We were at the back of the swimming pool complex in an area off-limits to students. Kasey had "borrowed" a key from her dad. The frozen fire ants were in their tub, stored inside an insulated picnic bag.

"If we get caught..."

She didn't have to finish the sentence. If we got caught, the consequences would be terrible. Death by tiger would seem like a slap on the wrist. "We'll just have to not get caught," I said, sounding much more confident than I felt.

I don't know why, but every time I'm about to do something that'll get me in trouble, a little voice in my head convinces me that *this time* everything will work out.

Today was no different.

"Everything will work out," I said. See?

Kasey opened a service door and we found ourselves inside the guts of the swimming pool, where all the pumps and pipes and ducts lived.

But we weren't interested in that stuff. What we were after was the changing rooms.

"This way," Kasey said, making a sharp left.

I followed her down a maze of concrete passageways. Above us, we could hear people taking their seats for the competition.

Kasey stopped outside a small door. "This

is where Principal Winton gets changed," she
whispered. "We have to be quick. In, out, no mess-
ups. But there's a chance Principal Winton will
be in the dressing room when we open the door. If
that happens, we're done for."

I nodded and gulped. "Let's do it."

What could possibly go wrong?

CHAPTER 49

PANIC IS DEFINITELY AN OPTION

The dressing room was empty.

I breathed a huge sigh of relief. HUGE.

What had seemed like a hilarious and totally genius idea outside was feeling a whole lot less hilarious and totally genius now that we were actually creeping around somewhere we shouldn't be.

"C'mon," Kasey whispered. The girl seemed to have absolutely zero fear.

I unzipped the picnic bag and placed it on one of the benches.

The dressing room was a small one, reserved for teachers. Even though Principal Winton wasn't in the race, he dressed like he was ready to dive in himself: He wore swim trunks under his regular clothes. The trunks were all hung up for him, neat and clean and perfect.

Kasey took the lid off the plastic tub. Reluctantly (like, really, *really* reluctantly), I picked up Principal Winton's swim trunks and found the little inside pocket on the waistband. I held it open and Kasey spooned in as many of the frozen ants as she could. I could see one or two of them beginning to move slowly. When all the ants were in, I put the swimming trunks back on the hanger.

"Okay," Kasey whispered. "Let's go."

She moved to the door and turned the handle, but it wouldn't open.

Kasey gave it a wiggle. Nothing.

"Is it locked?!" I hissed. I was starting to panic.

Kasey shook her head. "I think it's stuck."

She pulled at the door, but again it didn't budge. I heard voices, one of which was the unmistakable croak of the Velociraptor.

"We're trapped!" I squeaked, leaping directly to full-on freak-out.

"Stop panicking!" she hissed. "Panic is not an option!"

"Yes, it is!" I hissed back. You might've noticed we were doing a LOT of hissing and squeaking. "Panic is definitely an option and I'm taking it!"

Kasey ignored me, her eyes racing around the room for any means of escape. "In there!" she whispered, pointing to a locker. The dressing room was lined with floor-to-ceiling lockers fitted with slatted wooden doors, like venetian blinds.

"We'll never fit in th—"

Kasey shoved me inside and closed the door behind us.

I swiveled around just in time to see Principal Winton entering the room. Up until that point, I hadn't realized I could panic any more than I already was.

But watching Principal Winton walk toward us, I realized—

I could.

CHAPTER 50

SOMEONE CLEAN MY EYEBALLS

Stuck inside one of the dressing room lockers, with our only escape route cut off, we had no choice but to watch as Principal Winton began to get changed. I guess we could have closed our eyes, but somehow, like when you want to stop watching a horror movie but can't, we couldn't.

"Oh no…" I breathed as he began taking off his clothes. I don't know why this came as a shock.

I mean, there he was, inside a changing room. What *else* would he be doing?

Principal Winton took off his shoes and his socks.

He took off his jacket and shirt. He took off his tie.

He took off his pants and stood directly in front of us, wearing nothing but a pair of tighty-whities.

Kasey made a noise like she was going to be sick. I just hoped Principal Winton wouldn't take off his underwear.

Luckily, Kasey and I closed our eyes before we had to see anything else. Still, the sight of Principal Winton in his underwear had burned itself into my eyeballs forever. I was probably going to need therapy.

CHAPTER 51

OHSWEETPOTATOPIE!

I'll spare you any more description.

Thankfully, Principal Winton didn't stand around completely naked for long. He put on his swimming clothes (complete with trunks containing a secret stash of frozen fire ants), put his clothes on over them—fortunately he didn't look in the locker we were hiding in—and left.

We waited a few seconds and then spilled out of the locker.

I opened my mouth to speak, but Kasey stopped me.

"No," she said firmly. "*That* didn't happen, okay? We must never speak of this again. Is that understood?"

I nodded. The *last* thing I wanted to discuss was Principal Winton's undies.

Kasey tried the back door of the changing room, but it was still stuck. She moved to the main door and opened it a crack.

"All clear," she said, and we stepped out into the hallway.

We made our way unseen to the back of the hall, underneath the grandstand.

The place was pretty much full by now. Rows and rows of parents sat waiting for the races to begin. Since Kasey wasn't a student at BHP, it would have looked odd if she'd been in the audience.

I followed her through a maze of hallways and up some stairs until we emerged behind the electronic scoreboard. From here, we had a perfect view of the whole swimming pool. The place was buzzing with excitement and getting warm.

Warm enough to thaw a bunch of frozen ants. "There he is," Kasey said. She pointed to the end of the pool, where Principal Winton was standing on a small stage and holding a microphone.

"Ladies and gentlemen, boys and girls," he said in a clear, confident voice. It was the voice of someone used to being listened to, the voice of authority.

Everyone went quiet. Principal Winton was a man to be taken seriously.

"Welcome to another fantastic BHP swim meet, and a special welcome to—*yerk!*"

Not many people noticed that first little *yerk*, but Kasey and I did. We looked at each other and smirked.

Principal Winton shuffled uncomfortably on the podium. He waggled his rear end from side to side. A couple of the parents looked at each other, but so far no one had noticed anything much.

"Well, yes," Principal Winton continued, looking less sure of himself than he had two minutes ago. "As I was saying, BHP would like to welcome Woodland Middle School. We hope, as always, that—*Yerk! Ungh! Ho!*—that—*Yoicks! Woo! Hey, whoa!*—this will be a close—*Mwhayhay!*—match."

Now there was no doubt. Principal Winton's *yerk*s and *yoicks*es had been heard by plenty of people in the crowd, and to make things worse, he began twitching his left leg and jiggling his butt in a very noticeable way. Something very wrong was happening in Principal Winton's pants.

Mr. Fitzpatrick looked up at him and raised an eyebrow in question.

Principal Winton shrugged. *I don't know*, his face seemed to say. Recovering a little, he tried to continue as the crowd began to murmur. "So, erm, as I was, um, saying—NYAAAARGH! *HMMF!* *"OHSWEETPOTATOPIE!!!!!"*

There was no hiding it now.

"I'm terribly sorry, ladies and gentlemen," Principal Winton said. "I'm not sure exactly wh—HARR*OOOOOOOOO*HAAAA! HA*HAHAHAH*NNNNNGGG!"

Principal Winton was practically gyrating. His eyes bulged. His butt vibrated. His face turned a deep scarlet. He bit his lip. At one point it looked like he was disco dancing.

With a final, almost superhuman effort to keep things on track, Principal Winton smiled and turned back to the microphone. Sweat broke out on his forehead as he tried to ignore what was happening in his swimming trunks.

But both Kasey and I knew his efforts were doomed.

The ants had woken up.

CHAPTER 52

THINK OF THE CHILDREN!

Those fire ants must have been pretty angry.
Wouldn't you be, if you'd been dug up out of your house, frozen, and then inserted into a pair of unmentionables? If I were a fire ant in that situation, I would have started biting anything I could sink my ant fangs into.

Which, in this case, happened to be Principal Winton's butt cheeks.

Leaping from the podium like a man who has suddenly discovered that his pants are full of ants, Principal Winton spun wildly along the edge of the pool, ripping frantically at his clothes. Off came his sweater, his pants, and his shoes, until all that was left were his trunks. There was a collective gasp from the audience as everyone connected the dots and realized what was going to happen next. Sure enough, Principal Winton grabbed the edge of his trunks and—

"*No!*" a woman in the crowd screamed. "For the love of God, don't do it, Principal Winton! *Please!* THINK OF THE CHILDREN!"

It was too late.

Principal Winton was *not* thinking of the children. He wasn't thinking of BHP or the school board. His universe had shrunk down to one very simple, very important issue—getting rid of every single angry fire ant currently munching on the most delicate parts of his anatomy.

"AAAAARRRRGHHHHHHHHHNNNNGGGG!"
he screamed, ripping off his trunks. Suddenly,
shockingly, there was Principal Winton, naked,
gyrating in front of a thousand BHP parents,
students, and teachers.

A journalist from the local newspaper could
hardly believe his luck and began taking photos.
Eight zillion phones started recording the footage.
Holly Lindenberg's grandmother fainted, and
Henry Tamworth-Blythe—Cory's father—had to be
physically restrained. An elderly gentleman near
the back required defibrillation. The BHP Parent-
Teacher Association shook their heads before
walking out, while a small sixth grader in the front
row started to cry. Mr. Fitzpatrick and a bunch of
teachers circled the podium, waiting for a chance
to grab their wildly flailing boss. Everyone else in
the hall was...

    A. screaming;
    B. laughing;
    C. pointing;
    D. staring in disbelief; or
    E. doing all of the above.

Principal Winton didn't care. He really didn't. With his hands scrabbling frantically around his butt (and other butt-related areas), Principal Winton gave one last anguished howl and plunged into the water.

There was a stunned silence.

After a few seconds, Principal Winton's face popped back up. He spat out a mouthful of water and smiled a smile of complete and total bliss. The kind of smile that you will only see on the face of someone no longer being bitten by eight hundred angry ants.

But the Velociraptor's happiness didn't last long.

As the glow from his de-anting faded and he took in the crowd of shocked parents and near-hysterical students, his smile vanished. He groaned and slid back under the water.

There was no way this could get any worse.

It got worse.

Mr. Fitzpatrick dove in. *"I'll save you, boss!"* he screeched.

Kasey looked at me as though I were a magician. "Awesome," she breathed.

I didn't reply. I was too busy watching Mr. Fitzpatrick hauling Principal Winton up onto the side of the pool and performing CPR. I don't think he needed it, because his eyes were wide open. And call me paranoid, but they seemed to be staring through the electronic scoreboard and right at me.

I swallowed hard and stepped back into the shadows.

There was no way he could know this was because of me.

Absolutely no way. Right?

A NON-UNDERGROUND LAIR

I was in evil villain Dr. McNasty aka Principal Winton's secret underground lair—deceptively disguised as an ordinary school principal's office and (even more deceptively) not underground.

"I'm going to ask you one more time, Khatchadorian," he said while stroking the fluffy white cat on his lap. It's a well-known fact that all evil villains love fluffy white cats. Don't ask me why, they just do.

"Admit your part in this ant outrage, and Mr. Huggleberry and I will show mercy. Your end will be swift and painless. Resist or deny, and things will be rather unpleasant, I can assure you."

"I'll never talk, McNasty," I snarled, struggling against the ropes that held me in place, directly over a pit of bubbling lava. "You've got nothing to connect me to the ants! Nothing!"

Dr. McNasty gave Mr. Huggleberry a tickle under his chin and the cat purred. "That's where you're quite mistaken, Mr. Khatchadorian." McNasty nodded to his henchperson, Mr. Fitzpatrick aka Mustache. "Send in the informant!"

Mustache opened the door, and my archnemesis, Coldly Tiptoe-Burp, walked in.

"You!" I gasped.

Tiptoe-Burp bowed in front of McNasty. "Show

Mr. Khatchadorian what you showed me earlier, Mr. Tiptoe-Burp," McNasty said.

"Of course, Your Nastiness." Tiptoe-Burp bowed so low his nose scraped the carpet. He pulled a remote from his pocket and pointed it at the large TV on the wall. Tiptoe-Burp clicked and a video clip filled the screen. It was grainy and wobbly but still clear enough to show Kasey and me collecting the fire ants.

"I realized the prisoner was up to no good," Tiptoe-Burp said. "So I followed him."

"That doesn't prove anything," I argued, fighting against my restraints. "We could have been collecting them for a...a...science project! That doesn't prove we put the ants in Principal Winton's underpants."

Tiptoe-Burp moved on to another clip. Filmed through one of the dressing room locker doors, it showed me and Kasey putting the ants in Principal Winton's swim trunks.

My head slumped.

"That will be all, Mr. Tiptoe-Burp," Dr. McNasty said.

I watched the informant leave.

"Now," McNasty said, "all that remains is for me to decide your punishment."

"*I love this bit!*" Mustache yelled. Everything went black.

CHAPTER 54

A COOL MILLION

E xpelled?" Mom said. She looked exactly
62 percent worried, 16 percent annoyed,
14 percent angry, 7 percent *completely furious*, and
1 percent secretly proud. (Although it's possible
that last one was just me hoping.)

It was Monday night and we were in the
kitchen at 322 Chestnut Drive.

I nodded miserably.

"Let me get this straight," Mom said. "You
and Kasey put *spiders* in Principal Winton's
underwear?"

"His swim trunks," I corrected. "And they were
ants."

"Trunks, ants, underwear, whatever. And you
put the ants in because he gave you detention?"

I nodded again. "But also because he was going to bulldoze Kasey's house and I thought that wasn't right. Ants seemed like what he...deserved."

"Awesome," Georgia said. She actually looked impressed.

"Georgia, honey, please don't encourage him," Mom said, sighing. She put her hand to her head. "This is serious."

Mom was right. This *was* serious. And I was about to discover just how serious.

Mom paced up and down the kitchen. I made sure there were no heavy pans nearby. Even Jules Khatchadorian could reach a breaking point. Judging by the look on her face, we were at Mom Meltdown DEFCON 5 and rising. I had never seen her so upset.

Mom stopped in her tracks and turned to me. "You know what this means, Rafe?"

"Yes," I said. "I'll have to find another school or maybe go back home or—"

"No," Mom said slowly. "This means we don't get to keep the house."

I blinked. What?

"We don't get to keep the house?" Georgia wailed.

"That's right." Mom's anger had faded, and she just looked sad now. Which was, of course, a lot worse. I can cope with her being mad, but when she gets disappointed it burns me up.

"It looks like we're heading back to Hills Village with absolutely nothing except a few moldy paintings," she continued. "Uncle Grey's will only holds if Rafe finishes a semester."

I sagged miserably. How could I possibly have forgotten something so major? The truth was, I hadn't *really* forgotten. I just hadn't expected to be caught or expelled—they were only ants—but now I realized I'd messed everything up.

Again.

"But, but, but..." I stammered.

"But nothing, Rafe," Mom said. "That's it, game over. No house. No million dollars and back to Swifty's for me."

Listen, kids, here's a warning from me: if you ever get the urge to put frozen fire ants (or any other insect) into the underwear of an authority figure because they want to bulldoze your friend's house, DON'T.

It might cost you a million dollars.

CHAPTER 55

THINGS GET WORSE

Obviously, I was grounded. But I couldn't just sit there.

I *had* to find out what had happened to Kasey, who wasn't answering my texts. So, while Mom was working the phone, trying a million (oops, too soon?) ways to get around this expelling thing, and Georgia was up in her room (most likely making a voodoo doll of me), I snuck out and headed for Golden Blades. The Spitballers had practice and I wanted to make sure the mural was going to carry on after I'd left.

I loved that mural, and it looked like it might be the only decent thing to come out of what was turning into a nightmare.

If Kasey managed to finish it.

Plus, I really did want to check on how Kasey was doing. I'd tried to heap the blame on myself, but if I knew BHP, they would do *something* to punish Kasey.

CHAPTER 56

AND SUDDENLY BETTER

They fired Dad," Kasey said. "Tamworth-Blythe said if Dad couldn't control me, then he had no place in BHP. Fifteen years Dad's been at BHP and he's out, starting next semester. No house, no job. Nothing."

"Because of *ants*?" I sat down on the seat next to Kasey. The Spitballers barreled past in a whirl of wheels and pads and elbows. When it was quiet again I looked at Kasey. "I'm sorry. If I hadn't thought this up, none of it would have happened."

Kasey shrugged. "I was in on it, too, Rafe, just as much as you."

"If it helps, my family lost a million dollars."

Kasey sat upright. "What?"

I told her about getting expelled and Uncle Grey's will. Kasey listened, open-mouthed.

"A million bucks? Holy moly, Batman! That is *out* there! I mean, my dad will find another job and we'll get somewhere else to live but...A MILLION DOLLARS! Wow! That is serious cash! I mean, losing a million dol—"

"This isn't making me feel better."

The Spitballers came around again like a bunch of giant roller-skating wasps. When they'd gone, I saw Frost DeAndrews standing on the other side of the track.

He walked across the boards and hopped over the small fence separating the track from the seats. "You two look rather glum," he said, yawning. "I'd ask you what was the matter, but then you'd probably tell me, and I'm not really the sort of person who does *sympathy*." Frost DeAndrews pronounced the last word like you might say "manure" and wrinkled his nose in distaste.

Kasey jerked a thumb in my direction. "This guy just lost a million dollars."

Frost was amazed. "Really?"

Frost DeAndrews shows extreme amazement

Really?

I told him the story.

"A million dollars? Must be something about money in the air today," he said when I'd finished.

"Why?" asked Kasey.

"Oh well," Frost DeAndrews said, inspecting his nails, "Dee told me the Spitballers just found out that if they don't raise *half* a million dollars at the fundraiser and give it to Tamworth-Blythe Construction by next month, they're out. Golden Blades will close and become a highway. A frightful bore, isn't it?"

The three of us sat in a line with our heads in our hands.

Life *sucked*.

"Oh," Frost said, looking at me, "I forgot to

mention something about the paintings you showed me at your house. I did some checking around."

I shrugged. "And?"

"All of them are by your uncle," he said.

Gee, tell me something I don't know. I have to admit I was disappointed in Mr. DeAndrews.

"Yes, all except one," Frost added. "The big one over the mantelpiece might be a Bonini."

It took a few seconds for the information to sink in. "Wait," I said. "That's a *Bonini*? A genuine Franco Bonini?"

"No way!" Kasey gasped. "Really?"

Frost nodded. "Probably. It *was* signed by your uncle, but I have no idea why he did that. The painting is, I believe, a Bonini. I'll consult a friend who's an expert when she gets back from her vacation."

"Where's she on vacation?" I said. Information like this needed to be checked RIGHT NOW.

"Antarctica," Frost said.

"*Antarctica?* Who goes on vacation to Antarctica?"

"She does," Frost said. "But she's back in a week. I'll check then to see if it's genuine."

"And if it is?" I said. "How much would it be worth?"

"About half a million," Frost said. "Give or take."

CHAPTER 57

RECAP TIME

Okay, it's time for a recap.

Everyone get comfortable, take a deep breath, and let's go over what we know so far. There's been a lot going on—even by Rafe Khatchadorian standards—and today was proving to be something of a record. To lose a million dollars and then, less than four hours later, maybe *find* half a million dollars takes some doing. Everything was getting MUCH MORE COMPLICATED...if that's possible. This whole thing was, like our mural at Golden Blades, turning into a big mess. I need to get my head straight. It's time for some clear thinking. It's time for figuring things out. It's time for a list.

So here we go:

1. I'd definitely been expelled from BHP, which was bad because it meant that we would lose the house at 322 Chestnut Drive.

2. Kasey and her dad were getting booted out of their home.

3. But Frost DeAndrews discovered we might have a genuine Franco Bonini painting worth maybe a cool half million in the house at Chestnut Drive, which was the exact amount the Spitballers needed to save Golden Blades from demolition.

Even with the list, my head was spinning with all the information I was trying to keep track of, so I decided the best thing to do was for me to speak to the smartest person I know.

CHAPTER 58

MOM LOGIC

Mom might not have that many letters after her name (or any letters after her name). She's not a rocket scientist or a brain surgeon, she can't solve difficult math problems or speak eighteen languages while writing computer code, but here's the thing: Mom *knows* stuff.

Moms *always* know what to do and it always seems to work out somehow. It sometimes makes no kind of sense whatsoever, but at the same time it makes perfect sense.

So, anyway, the half a mill was still only a maybe, but it was a maybe from Frost DeAndrews, Australia's greatest art critic.

It was a chance.

CHAPTER 59

1972 AND ALL THAT

When I got to Chestnut Drive, I began babbling before Mom had a chance to remember that, technically, I was grounded. "Rafe, slow down," Mom said, directing me to a chair. "Here, sit. You too, Georgia. I've got some news I need to talk to both of you about."

Mom had that serious Mom tone in her voice, so Georgia and I sat down at the kitchen table. We had come to a sort of truce because all this grown-up stuff was happening. She did still have that voodoo doll.

"I made some phone calls after you snuck off to the stadium," Mom said.

I looked at her in surprise. "You knew about me sneaking off?"

"I know everything, honey," Mom said pityingly.

Then she waved a hand and continued. "So, as I was saying, I made some phone calls, checking on the house stuff, and I found out a few things."

"Like what?" Georgia asked warily.

Mom took a deep breath and began. "Uncle Grey did leave you the house, but what Mr. Ato conveniently didn't mention was that, once you'd finished at BHP, although we *could* sell the house, we would have to sell it to the city council."

"So?" I couldn't see what the problem was. We'd still get the money.

"At 1972 prices," Mom added. "Which is exactly two thousand dollars."

"Two thousand dollars?!" Georgia and I said in unison.

Mom nodded.

"So it didn't really matter much if I got expelled?"

Mom nodded again. "Exactly. It mattered about two thousand dollars, I guess."

"Wow." Uncle Grey had been seriously weird.

At 1972 prices? Real Franco Boninis and maybe fake Franco Boninis?

"Yes, wow," Mom said.

"Wow," Georgia said.

The three of us sat in silence while we tried to figure out if we'd had good luck or bad luck.

"What else did you find out?" I asked. "You said you'd found out a few things."

"Well, I found out we do own all the stuff in the house." Mom laughed. "Like it's worth anything."

My eyes strayed to the big painting over the mantelpiece, and I began to smile.

"What?" Mom said, trying to see what I was looking at.

So I told her.

CHAPTER 60

JUST THIS ONCE

We did it," Kasey said, stepping back with her hands on her hips.

"Not quite." I dipped my brush in a pot of blue paint and added a tiny dot. "There. Now we're done."

Kasey gave me a playful shin-kick for old times' sake. I didn't mind; the bruise would be a reminder when our flight took off in a couple of days.

That's right, the Khatchadorians were heading back to Hills Village. The house at 322 Chestnut Drive had been sold to the city for two thousand dollars, and the best of Uncle Grey's paintings were on their way home. We didn't know what we were going to do with them, but it didn't seem right to just sling them onto the trash heap. The Bonini painting was at an art dealer's gallery, waiting for the arguments about who owned it to settle. Mom was actually there today, supposedly sorting it out once and for all. Georgia was with us at Golden Blades, pitching in almost like a regular human being.

Kasey and I moved way back so we could finally see the whole mural.

It was great, even if I did say so myself.

A great big, blobby, wiggly-wobbly mess dancing across the wall of the old stadium. It might not have been a Bonini, but it was a giant improvement on what had been there before.

Which, considering there'd been nothing there before, maybe wasn't saying much.

It was the day of the Spitballers fundraiser, the last day of Golden Blades Stadium, if Henry Tamworth-Blythe had anything to do with it.

There was a line of bulldozers already parked just outside the stadium fence, waiting for the signal to come in and start knocking things down.

Right now, it didn't look like there was a whole lot we could do about it, but we were determined to go out with a real bang. The posters had been posted all over town for the past week.

A sold-out crowd of six thousand had paid more than a hundred thousand dollars for tickets, but it looked like that wasn't going to be enough, even if we sold a ton of burgers.

"Tamworth-Blythe bought fifty tickets," Kasey said. "Dee told me he wanted to be here when the last whistle blew so he could personally swing the first sledgehammer at midnight. The whole crew will be down there—Cory and his cronies, Principal Winton, Mr. Fitzpatrick—all gloating."

"Something will turn up," I said.

Kasey smiled sadly. "Thanks, Socks, but I don't think so. Life doesn't work that way."

I knew that. Still, looking at our great big mural dancing along the walls of Golden Blades Stadium, I couldn't help thinking that maybe this time it would.

Just this once.

KER-RUNCH TIME!

★ Come see the LA Spitballers pulverize the Pasadena Pirates! ★

In a jaw-dropping, eye-popping, body-crunching Rock-and-Rolling Roller Derby END-OF-THE-ROAD EXTRAVAGANZA!

CHAPTER 61

KER-RUNCH!

Dee Stroyer, looking like she meant business, curved down the bank at one end of the stadium and took out two Pasadena Pirates in one collision. "Go, Lola!" she yelled as a gap opened up in front of Lola the Roller.

Lola pushed hard for the gap, knocking an incoming Pasadena Pirate to one side and gaining ground on the opposing jammer. (It's a roller derby term. Google it; it'll be quicker.)

The crowd roared when Lola swept past the Pirate just as the clock ticked down to the two-minute mark. The scoreboard notched up a point and the LA Spitballers took the lead for the first time.

The End-of-the-Road Extravaganza was

going great, and the crowd was jumping. There was music and lasers and indoor fireworks—all donated by friends and relatives of the Spitballers. The only buzzkill was the sight of Henry and Cory Tamworth-Blythe, Principal Winton, Mr. Fitzpatrick, and the rest of the wrecking crew on the finish line in the best seats in the house. Henry Tamworth-Blythe hadn't been kidding about wanting to be the first to start smashing up Golden Blades. The guy really had brought his own sledgehammer.

I was down in the Spitballers' pit in the center of the track along with a bunch of Spitballer coaches. I scanned the crowd for Mom but couldn't see her anywhere. Georgia was sitting in the front row with some of her school friends and their parents.

"Where's Mom?" I mouthed. It was unlike her to miss an event like this.

Georgia shrugged.

The whistle blew to mark the end of the jam, and the teams skated in toward their benches.

As the music started, I moved away to let the team talk tactics. Kasey skated past and gave me a friendly shove with her shoulder pad.

"Is this awesome or what?!" she yelled.

"Fantastic!" I replied, rubbing my shoulder.

Kasey skated over to her team, looking as happy as I could remember seeing her. The Spitballers were truly PULVERIZING the Pasadena Pirates. If only *this* whole place weren't going to be pulverized at midnight by the Tamworth-Blythes.

I looked across at Cory. He patted the sledgehammer and smiled. Principal Winton shuffled uncomfortably on his special doughnut-shaped butt cushion and gave me a full-on laser death stare. Mr. Fitzpatrick twirled his mustache aggressively. There wouldn't be any last-minute sympathy coming from that bunch. There would be no rescue, no daring escape. Golden Blades was doomed.

I swallowed hard and looked up at the stadium clock.

One hour to go.

CHAPTER 62

MOM? MOM? MOM!

The hour raced past in a blur of skates and shouts and music. The crowd was loving it, but it was hard not to feel the end coming closer with every passing second.

The final whistle blew, the band blasted one last power chord, two jets of sparks erupted from funnels at either side of the track, and glittery confetti fell from the ceiling.

It was done. We'd tried our best, but Golden Blades was doomed.

Kasey skated across, her face flushed with excitement.

"Champ!" I said, grinning.

She pumped a fist to the sky in a sort of cool, ironic way. "Yay."

It had been a great night, but we both knew there wouldn't be any more. By tomorrow night, Golden Blades and our mural would be on their way to dust.

The Tamworth-Blythe crew were exchanging high fives.

"Those guys make me sick," Kasey said, looking more like the Egg Girl I'd met a month or so back. "I'd love to kick those boneheads right in the breadbaskets, every last one of them."

I wasn't exactly sure what or where a breadbasket was, but it sounded painful.

"Here they come," I said.

Cory and his perfect hair led the way into the middle of the track, closely followed by two of his most repulsive sidekicks and then the rest of the suit-wearing, slimy bunch, with Henry T-B bringing up the rear. He was trying on the sledgehammer for size.

The crowd started booing and whistling loud enough to raise the roof of the old place. Henry Tamworth-Blythe didn't care. He strutted toward the microphone on the small stage as objects rained down.

It was one minute to midnight when Tamworth-Blythe spoke into the mic. "Silence!" he yelled. He raised the sledgehammer high above his head. "In exactly one minute, the process of ridding our city of this pile of filth and chaos will begin!" Henry paused as the boos increased in volume.

When he could make himself heard, he spoke again. "Boo, all YOU losers! The stadium is ours! Soon it will be under ten feet of fine concrete, and your little games and murals will be distant memories! There's no place for this kind of unreg—"

"Hold it right there, buster!" a familiar voice yelled.

"Oh! Em! Gee!" Kasey elbowed me in the ribs.

Through my pain I turned to see my MOM skating through the crowd—yes, skating—straight at Tamworth-Blythe. For some completely unknown reason, she was dressed like one of the Pasadena Pirates. Then, with a shock, I realized she WAS one of the Pasadena Pirates!

CHAPTER 63

NO TRESPASSING!

Mom!" I yelped. "Why are…*what*…I mean…
huh?"

Okay, it wasn't great, I admit. And Mom clearly
didn't think so either, because she just waved me
away impatiently.

"No time to waste!" she said, breezing past.

Henry Tamworth-Blythe flinched as Mom
skidded expertly to a stop with her nose about an
inch from his.

"Not so fast, bud!" she hissed, holding up five or
six sheets of paper.

Tamworth-Blythe took a step back and
nervously brushed his perfectly manicured hand
over his perfect hair. "What's this nonsense?" he
demanded.

"Aha!" Mom barked, and Tamworth-Blythe took
another step back. "These," Mom said, rattling
the papers in the air, "are the deed to Golden
Blades Stadium. As of eight o'clock tonight, the LA
Spitballers *own* Golden Blades, NOT you! So ditch
the hammer and get out of this stadium. You're
trespassing!"

"What!" spat Tamworth-Blythe.

"What?" screeched Principal Winton.

"What?" I gasped.

"What?" the entire crowd said in unison. (Which
was pretty impressive, to be honest.)

"I like cake!" Mr. Fitzpatrick declared, seeming to have trouble concentrating.

"Impossible!" Tamworth-Blythe sputtered. He snatched the papers from Mom's hand. "I have the best lawyers in the city right here! Let's see what *they* have to say about this."

Six of Tamworth-Blythe's entourage stepped forward. They were all dressed in identical suits.

"This is the entire firm of Bloot, Koot, Newt, Spoot, Van Den Hauwe, and Smith," Tamworth-Blythe said, smirking. He passed the papers to his lawyers, who gathered around in a tight huddle.

While they pointed and shrugged and talked, the rest of us waited in awkward silence.

"Loser," Cory Tamworth-Blythe said.

"Dimwit," I said back.

We both settled back into the awkward silence.

In books and movies, there aren't that many awkward silences, but in real life there are tons. And this one was a doozy. With six thousand spectators, this was one REALLY awkward silence.

Bloot, Koot, Newt, Spoot, Van Den Hauwe, and Smith eventually finished the inspection of

Mom's papers and whispered something in Henry Tamworth-Blythe's ear.

He turned bright red. "What?" he spat. "THEY own this dump?"

"That's correct, Mr. Tamworth-Blythe," Koot said. "There's no doubt."

Tamworth-Blythe looked as if he was going to pass out, and what Mom said next did nothing to help.

"And another thing, Toejam-Blurt," Mom said. "That painting you're so proud of up in the Great Hall? The Big Spaghetti Blobamacallit? That is NOT a Bonini!"

"What?" Tamworth-Blythe reeled. "Not a Bonini? That's impossible! Any art critic will tell you that is a genuine Bonini!"

Mom put two fingers to her mouth and whistled—see, right there was another thing I never knew about her—and Frost DeAndrews stepped out of the crowd. He flipped open a leather wallet and flashed a gold badge in Tamworth-Blythe's astonished face.

"My name is Frost DeAndrews, of the FBAAC—the Federal Bureau of Australian Art Critics," he said. "I am the most famous and most respected art critic in all of Australia, and that big mess in BHP I looked at today is just that—a big mess. It was, I suggest, probably painted by Grey Khatchadorian, which was likely the reason he'd been taken off the school board by Principal Winton's grandfather, who'd kept the fact that the painting was fake a secret ever since. If that's a Bonini, my name is Susan." DeAndrews paused and narrowed his eyes. "And my name is *not* Susan."

Tamworth-Blythe looked at him in horror. "But, but, but, but…"

"Keep doing that impression of a motor scooter and putt-putt back to Beverly Hills," Mom said.

I was impressed. "Good line, Mom."

Mom winked. "I've been practicing."

CHAPTER 64

CAPTAIN EXPOSITION STRIKES AGAIN!

Before we move on to the next bit, I don't think it's right to carry on without doing some explaining.

I got all this info *later*, understand? But since this is me telling you the story *now*, I thought I'd fill you in on some puzzling deets— like how my mom came to be a Pasadena Pirate. If this were a movie, there would be a real quick collection of short shots showing exactly what happened. So:

1. Mom took the Bonini painting to a dealer, where she found out it was worth half a mill, BUT...

2. Uncle Grey had worked his reverse magic on us again. Mom found out there was some really, really small print in the will that meant, for some weird reason, we could only sell the painting if we donated the money to a charity. We could NOT keep the money ourselves (no, I have no idea why, either), so...

3. (and this was the really clever part) Mom called Ms. Bennett and they had the Spitballers registered as a youth charity that helps troubled local kids learn how to play roller derby.

4. Mom sold the painting to the dealer and then donated the money from the painting to the Spitballers, who then bought Golden Blades Stadium. Ta-da!

5. Oh, and Mom had been training with the Pirates since we'd arrived. That's where she'd been when I thought she was spending all that time shopping or at the spa. She was already a really good skater, but I'd never bothered to find out. She had chosen the Pirates because she didn't want to spoil my fun hanging out with Kasey.

That was pretty nice of her, because it would've been kinda weird to have Mom there every time we'd gone to Golden Blades. And that was when...

6. Ms. Bennett got her brother, Frost DeAndrews, to take a look at the Big Spaghetti Blob.

Everyone got that? It's a lot to take in, right?

I STILL don't understand most of it, but just go with it, otherwise it'll make your brain hurt.

Sometimes stuff isn't simple, or all neatly wrapped up like a movie. Sometimes stuff is *messy*.

Okay, back to the action...

CHAPTER 65

SPEECHLESS

For probably the first time in his rich, perfect, easy life, Henry Tamworth-Blythe didn't know what to say.

He'd been outmaneuvered, outplayed, and out-thought by a secret roller-skating mom from Hills Village. And he had absolutely no idea how. In Henry Tamworth-Blythe's world, things like this simply did not happen. Henry Tamworth-Blythe had people whose sole job was to stop things like this from happening. Lawyers, accountants, parents, teachers, you name it—everyone around Henry Tamworth-Blythe had only one aim: to keep Henry happy.

Unfortunately, no one inside Golden Blades Stadium except Henry Tamworth-Blythe's little

entourage could care less about keeping Henry
Tamworth-Blythe happy.

With a howl of pure joy, the crowd chased
Henry Tamworth-Blythe and his entourage out of
the stadium. Someone must have found the cans of
spare paint from the mural, because the last thing
I saw was all the Henry Tamworth-Blythe people
covered in multicolored paint and running straight
back to Beverly Hills.

It was another glorious, great big paint-
splattered mess.

CHAPTER 66

OH, HILLS VILLAGE TANDOORI TEMPLE, HOW I DO LOVE THEE

So we're back home.

Back in Hills Village. Back at school and back to reality.

We're exactly ZERO dollars richer, but hey, did you ever seriously think the Khatchadorians would come out of this with a fortune?

Didn't think so. Things like that—being given great big wads of money—just doesn't *happen* to our kind of people.

But as I sat on my old bed, with Junior sniffing at the last stubborn scraps of Golden Blades mural paint in my hair, and me listening to Georgia and Grandma Dotty sing along to some dumb singer on the TV, and smelling the celebration homecoming takeout Mom had brought back from Tandoori Temple, I'll tell you this: I wouldn't swap places with the Cory Tamworth-Blythes of this world for a million dollars.

Okay, maybe for a million.

Let's call it half a mill.

"RAFE!" Mom called from downstairs.
"CURRY!"

I headed for the stairs, passing three of Uncle Grey's paintings (remember we'd shipped 'em out?).

Fifty grand and a ticket back to Beverly Hills. I can't say fairer than that.

Okay, ten Gs.

Six? Five hundred? Eight bucks and a strawberry milkshake?

"RAFE!"

ABOUT THE AUTHORS

JAMES PATTERSON is the most popular storyteller of our time. He is the creator of unforgettable characters and series, including Maximum Ride, Middle School, Treasure Hunters, and Jacky Ha-Ha. He holds the Guinness World Record for the most #1 *New York Times* bestsellers, and his books have sold more than 400 million copies worldwide. He has received an Edgar Award, nine Emmy Awards, the Literarian Award from the National Book Foundation, and the National Humanities Medal.

A tireless champion of the power of books and reading, Patterson created a children's book imprint, JIMMY Patterson, whose mission is simple: "We want every kid who finishes a JIMMY book to say, 'PLEASE GIVE ME ANOTHER BOOK.'" He has donated more than three million books to students and soldiers and funds over four hundred Teacher and Writer Education Scholarships at twenty-one colleges and universities. He also supports forty thousand school libraries and has donated millions of dollars to independent bookstores. Patterson invests proceeds from the sales of JIMMY Patterson Books in pro-reading initiatives.

MARTIN CHATTERTON was born in Liverpool, England, and has been successfully writing and illustrating books for almost thirty years. He has written dozens of children's books and illustrated many more for other writers, including several British Children's Laureates. His work has been published in fourteen languages and has won and been shortlisted in numerous awards in the UK, the United States, and Australia. Alongside writing for children, Martin writes crime fiction (as Ed Chatterton), continues to work as a graphic designer, and is currently working on his PhD. After time spent in the US, Martin now divides his time between Australia and the UK.

JOMIKE TEJIDO is an author-illustrator who has illustrated more than one hundred children's books. He is based in Manila and once got into trouble in school for passing around funny cartoons during class. He now does this for a living and shares his jokes with his daughters, Sophia and Fuji.

MIDDLE SCHOOL

- The Worst Years of My Life
- Get Me Out of Here!
- Big Fat Liar
- How I Survived Bullies, Broccoli, and Snake Hill
- Ultimate Showdown
- Save Rafe!
- Just My Rotten Luck
- Dog's Best Friend
- Escape to Australia
- From Hero to Zero
- Born to Rock
- Master of Disaster
- Field Trip Fiasco
- It's a Zoo in Here!
- Winter Blunderland
- Million Dollar Mess

TREASURE HUNTERS

- Treasure Hunters
- Danger Down the Nile
- Secret of the Forbidden City
- Peril at the Top of the World
- Quest for the City of Gold
- All-American Adventure
- The Plunder Down Under
- The Ultimate Quest
- The Greatest Treasure Hunt

MIDDLE GRADE FICTION

- Becoming Muhammad Ali (cowritten with Kwame Alexander)
- Best Nerds Forever
- Laugh Out Loud
- Minerva Keen's Detective Club
- Not So Normal Norbert
- Pottymouth and Stoopid
- Public School Superhero
- Scaredy Cat
- Unbelievably Boring Bart
- Word of Mouse

MAX EINSTEIN

- The Genius Experiment
- Rebels with a Cause
- Max Einstein Saves the Future
- World Champions!

For exclusives, trailers, and more about the books, visit Kids.JamesPatterson.com.